HEARTLAND TREASURES

An Anthology of Short Stories

Compiled and Edited by
Krystine Kercher and Jan Verhoeff

Heartland Treasures is a work of fictional short stories. Names, characters, locations, and places included in this book are strictly fictional, products of the authors' imaginations used fictionally. Any resemblance to real events, characters, or locations are strictly accidental and entirely coincidental.

Copyright @ Jan Verhoeff – 2020
All rights reserved.

No portion of this book may be reproduced in any form or by any electronic or mechanical means, including information storage and retrieval systems, without the express permission from the author, except by a reviewer who may quote brief passages in reviews.

Published in the United States of America
by JV Publications
www.JVPublications.com

Short Stories are Published based on Feature Use Rights
Compiled and Edited by
Krystine Kercher and Jan Verhoeff

Heartland Treasures
An Anthology of Short Stories
1st Edition, January 2020

ISBN: 9781660328550

Printed in the UNITED STATES OF AMERICA
2 4 6 8 0 9 7 5 3 1

Cover Photo by Gerhard Gellinger
Cover Design and Illustration by Krystine Kercher
Layout by Krystine Kercher

Acknowledgements Page

When a photo inspires you to create a cover, and open up a project to collect, gather, edit, and cultivate short stories and essays from a number of authors to fill up the pages inside the cover, you know there's just something about that photo. Gerhard Gellinger's photo of balloons dancing on summer breezes over a golden wheat field took me back to childhood when I would curl up on a blanket in the afternoon and watch the clouds drift overhead. In what was unbeknownst to him, Gerhard's photo began an undertaking that has overtaken my life for the past two years. I'll be forever grateful for his photo, the inspiration, and the challenge he brought me on that wistful winter morning.

Then, in a moment of weakness, inspiration, or caffeinated overindulgence, I threw out the invitation to a group of authors, inviting them to participate in the anthology I was about to create. One specific author replied with encouragement, and I entangled her into my dream, bringing her on as co-author/editor of the book. I'm forever grateful for the hundreds of hours she spent editing, collaborating, rewriting, polishing, reviewing, and formatting this massive project. Krystine Kercher, through all her frustration with me (I can be quite the problem child given the opportunity), and various writers along the way, has done an amazing job of pulling the stories together and putting them all into the proverbial basket of a hot air balloon to gain altitude and visibility in this amazing anthology of authors, stories, and concepts.

While Krystine and I both fought off illness and became overwhelmed with the project, her daughter Maria Kercher, jumped in and saved the day with an organizational concept that pulled the stories together in an interesting format, and compiled them into a single file – easier to shuttle back and forth between computers – and gave us motivation to carry on and complete the project. Did I mention how grateful we are for our little trouble-maker? We love her and appreciate her way more than she realizes.

That's not even all…

Heidi Kortman offered her services as a proof reader and came through like a champ! She caught our spelling and grammatical errors, fixed our punctuation, and made suggestions for edits when she found our duplicated paragraphs and errors. (Don't tell anyone that Compilers and Editors make mistakes! Oh, so embarrassing!) We are so grateful for all her hard work and effort on behalf of Heartland Treasures.

One of our authors from the earliest moment of the concept creation continued motivating, encouraging, and cajoling me into the process of completing this book. David Dockter, your continuous phone calls and encouragement, although at times I struggled to just keep being positive and upbeat about even getting the job done, kept me focused on publishing the final project. I joked at one point about you being a thorn in my side, but your phone calls and encouragement were ALWAYS appreciated.

I'm sure I'm leaving out a good many people along the way, whom I should be including in this acknowledgement. Krystine's parents come to mind, as do my family, many friends, and writers who asked about the project along the way, and a few others who offered interesting, if not helpful advice as we gathered stories… And one incredibly kind woman who asked what I was working on at midnight while I sat with her only hours before she succumbed to the coma that eventually took her life.

And of course, you, our reader who will be amazed, saddened, warmed, and challenged by the stories between these covers. Thank you for reading our stories.

Anthology Team

Editors

Krystine Kercher
Maria Kercher
Jan Verhoeff

Proof Reader

Heidi Kortman

Writers

John Davis
David Dockter
Oris George
Krystine Kercher
Heidi Kortman
Jude Kandace Laughe
Lisa M. Prysock
E.V. Sparrow
Jan Verhoeff
Mishael Witty

Cover Photo

Gerhard Gellinger

Publication

JVPublication/WriterThoughts
www.JVPublications.com
www.WriterThoughts.com

Table of Contents

Foreword ix

Cold Eggs, Hot Coffee, Warm Heart..............1

Homeless on Fisher Peak 10

Not Even Solomon 25

Competing for the Hearty Hearth 34

Bringing Granny Home..................................49

Cactus Justice 62

To Fly A Balloon...70

A Man Full-Grown and His Donkey............77

Apple River Bride 95

Balloons at Sunrise 118

Susan's Angry Again 125

South Dakota Foreman..................................143

Dalliance 167

Grizzly Escape 192

The Whisker Dilemma..................................198

Access, Hash Browns, Cherry Pie................226

About the Authors 237

Foreword

From Tia's cry, "They're hurting the bunnies!" to the loathsome laughter of George, and Doc Flannery's "I'm looking for a distraction." A thrill runs through me when readers share these memorable quotes, a few well known writers, and pages of heart-stopping suspense.

Before I tell you what's inside, I want to say thank you for taking time to check into the pages of these Heartland treasures.

You'll experience gut-wrenching sorrow, belly laughs, and tears as you wander through this maze of well-written short stories. Page after page of Heartland treasures reveal time honored and memorable adventures, legends, and chronicles.

Which story from our pages will you share?

Will it be the thieves who fell face first into a bed of cactus? Or the rain on Fisher Peak? Cherry Pie at Charlie's diner? You might even find the story you most relate to somewhere within the walls of Giggie's bookstore?

With balloons lifting on invisible breezes to drift high above the city, we opened our pages for a sprinkling of fancy, a bit of romance, and some tales of woe and displeasure. Between these pages, you'll find heartwarming slices of life that entertain.

Travel back in time to the prairie, or through a tangled moment of memories, a story of fishing with dad, or a fulfilling dream almost forgotten... Wherever you find yourself, the authors of this book, and our dear editorial specialist, Maria Kercher, pray that you carry a story with you. Keep the story in your heart, treasure it in the book, and share it from memory, or from the pages.

Take time to fall in love with characters, meet a few new writers, and get lost scenes you'll want to visit.

Fisher's Peak comes to mind. You'll fall head over heels in love with the town on the Colorado - New Mexico Border packed with quaint charm and history. Appreciate the pleasure of drifting on the breeze of an early dawn, acknowledging God's creation under the brow of a hot air balloon. You don't suppose they landed in a wheat field, now... Do you?

So, I told ole Oris I finished editing this book, and asked him if he wanted the readers to know anything specific, and he said, "If you can't go fishin', just find a spot in the sun and curl up with a good book. Either one'll grow whiskers on yer chin and hair on yer legs."

There you have it...

Please, come along and grow whiskers on your chin or hair on your legs...

Read a good book with us.

Jan Verhoeff

Cold Eggs, Hot Coffee, Warm Heart
Heidi Kortman

"Charlie, I'll stop for breakfast by 4:00 tomorrow morning, but I'll grab and run." Doc Dennis crushed the paper napkin, dropping it beside his plate on the worn green diner counter. "Make my order 'to go'."

"Can do, Doc." Charlie flipped another customer's order of "two over-easy," and grabbed the marker for the whiteboard. In a practiced spin, he left the notation of Doc's standing order then pulled toast onto the other customer's plate beside steaming eggs.

He slid Doc's debit card down the slot in the machine, waited for the receipt to spool out, and ripped it free. He shoved the slip across the counter. Doc flattened it to scrawl his name on the line.

"Thanks, Charlie."

3:55 the next morning. Charlie never knew, on "grab and run" days, where Doc Dennis headed. Now, Doc's breakfast waited above the grill in a Styrofoam box. A blast of cold air preceded squeaking footsteps. Charlie turned away from the hash browns and grabbed the box. "Here you go, Doc."

"Since when do I order a burger 'to go', Charlie?" Mitch said.

"Sorry, thought you were Doc." He put the box back, and slapped a beef patty on the grill. "You want onion?"

"Always."

A siren's wail interrupted them. Charlie snatched the box—4:05 a.m. Container in hand, he faced the counter. Marianne tugged at her scarf. Snow slid down her hair.

"Coffee, Charlie, quick." She shivered. "They finally got him loaded. Took them long enough—it's so cold. Hope he makes it."

He set the container on the shelf, poured coffee, and rearranged the crisping potatoes. "What happened, Marianne?"

"Guy in a Red Sox jacket stepped between cars to cross the street—plow clipped him. What a mess." Her hands shook as she lifted the cup. "I stayed until the paramedics came, covered him with my coat, you know." She swallowed and sighed. "This is the best coffee, Charlie. The guy screamed and panted, 'God, bless the kids on the ward.' "

Charlie dropped the spatula.

Maybe it wasn't Doc. He could breeze in any minute, glad for the breakfast in the box. Yesterday, he'd been early. Charlie dared ask why he bent his head over the plate.

"I pray for the kids on my ward, Charlie. Cancer is scary. I thank God for you, too."

"For me? Why?"

"Feeding people is good work. Jesus fed thousands, because hungry people can't pay attention."

This morning, Charlie's job had seemed important. He grabbed another spatula, slid the meat onto a bun with a generous dollop of grilled onion.

"Great burger," Mitch grunted around a mouthful.

Hot grease burned Charlie's hand—he'd rapped the spatula on the grill too hard. "Did he have red hair, Marianne?" Please, not Doc.

"Dunno. He wore a stocking cap. I talked to him, but he didn't seem to realize I was there. Blood on the snow…" Marianne shuddered, and stared down into the mug. "I wish that streetlight had been farther away." She finished her coffee and dropped change from her pocket on the counter.

Charlie scraped Marianne's payment into one palm, took Mitch's cash, and sorted everything into the till—4:15 a.m.

The beat-cop tossed a buck on the counter. Charlie poured coffee. "Bill, did you see that guy hit by the plow?"

"Nope."

Charlie shoved scorched potatoes into the trash and discarded Doc's cold eggs—he deserved fresh food. He paced. Snow blurred the people outside. None of them moved like Doc. Cooking more eggs made no sense until Charlie knew where Doc was.

He dumped grounds from pot number one, and refilled it. Soon, the off-duty cabbies would arrive for coffee, and wedges of pie. Charlie scraped grease from the grill. Every sound that penetrated the plate glass window distracted him.

As he sprayed the countertop between customers, the compressions of the trigger reminded him of Marianne's description of the victim's panting—4:28. "Bless the kids on the ward," Charlie muttered. They needed it, but he sure hoped Doc didn't.

"Eddie, you're first today," Charlie called, over the sounds of perking coffee and sleet spattering the window. The cabbie yanked off his leather gloves.

"Nasty one today. Something happened a couple blocks north. I drove through a patch of bloody snow in the middle of the street—didn't see an ambulance."

Charlie thumped a mug before the cabbie, and groped for the half-full carafe, his attention focused on the street.

"Watch it, Charlie." The cabbie snatched his copy of the Boston Globe away from puddling coffee, and shifted to a different barstool.

The nurse's shoes squelched in the snowmelt on the floor. "Do you know Doc Dennis?" Charlie said.

"Dennis who?" she said.

"I don't know his last name, but he's gangly, has red hair, and treats kids for cancer."

"I work in obstetrics, so I'm afraid I can't help you." She took the seat beyond the cabbie. "Scrambled eggs and whole wheat toast, please."

Charlie swallowed hard. Her order matched Doc's. "Yes, Ma'am, coming right up," he replied, and turned to the grill. 5:00—Doc's an hour late.

"Should hit the road," Eddie said, and flipped a bill on the counter. George Washington's hair absorbed coffee like dye.

Charlie's grease burn had blistered, and he gripped the nurse's plate gingerly. He set the food in front of her, and tried to ignore the stinging. As he turned away, Charlie shook his wrist.

"Did you burn yourself?" she said.

"It's not bad." Charlie spread bacon on the grill, grabbed a fistful of paper towel, and then moved Eddie's dollar from the pool of coffee on the counter. He blotted up the spill before covering the already rippling money with another sheet of toweling.

When the currency was merely damp, he dropped it on top of the stack in the cash drawer, and flipped the wire down.

"Those eggs hit the spot, Charlie." The nurse yawned then bit into her jam-smeared toast. She chewed while opening her purse to pay. "Have that burn looked at. Don't break the blister."

He dropped in her bills and quarters, and shut the cash register drawer — 5:15. Charlie flipped the bacon. More grease spattered his wrist. He could stand pain, but Doc hadn't stopped for his breakfast, and Doc was more reliable even than Mitch. Mass General stood a few blocks away. Charlie felt sure Doc worked there.

He shut off the grill, flipped the light switch, and turned the sign on the door to "Closed" for the second time in ten years — a good record.

Charlie jammed his fist into the sleeve of his jacket. The blisters tore. Wetness stuck his hand to the lining—too late for ice, now.

Gritting his teeth, he forced his hand past the elastic in the cuff.

Charlie wrapped his hand in a clean towel, pressing the flap of skin on the raw flesh. Marianne said the man panted, screamed, and prayed. Charlie understood why, but he shivered at the memory.

Please, let the first person he saw at Mass General be Doc Dennis.

Charlie slipped and skidded along the sleet-covered sidewalk but he couldn't move any slower. Even more than relief for his burns, he wanted to know Doc was okay. Another ambulance passed. If he didn't find Doc, he'd try another hospital.

Maybe Doc stayed at the hospital all night, with one of the kids. "It'll be grab and run," he remembered, and knew it wasn't so. God bless the kids on the ward, especially if they faced the day without Doc Dennis.

Charlie entered the ER. An intern with a clipboard met him.

"Name?" The man's eyes barely left the form in his hand.

"I'm Charlie Harrigan." He scanned the room—no sign of Doc Dennis.

"Do you have insurance, Mr. Harrigan?"

"Yes, but this is more important. Do you know Doc Dennis, who treats kids for cancer?" Charlie relaxed his grip on the towel. It slipped, pulling the loose skin back. He gritted his teeth as the air flamed across raw flesh.

"You'll have to show your card. How did you injure yourself?"

"A grease burn." Charlie dug out his wallet. "Please, do you know Doc Dennis?" he asked.

"I haven't worked in pediatric oncology, Mr. Harrigan. Take a seat here."

The intern pulled a curtain aside. Charlie stepped through.

As he balanced the clipboard on his knee, and struggled to fill in the blanks on the form with his towel-wrapped hand, he heard women's voices beyond the curtain that enclosed him.

"What a shame. Dr. Flannery's still in surgery."

"Looked bad when they brought him in. He might lose a leg."

Charlie dropped the pen and clipboard. A woman's hand pulled the curtain aside.

"Are you having problems?" She bent, and gathered the items.

"Please, will you tell me if the Doctor Flannery you mentioned has red hair? Does he treat kids for cancer?" He accepted the pen and clipboard.

"Is one of his patients your child?" She tilted her head to one side and waited.

Charlie shook his head.

"Then I'm not allowed to give information," she said.

"Wait, Miss. When they brought Doctor Flannery in, was he praying for the kids?"

"How could you know he does that?" She stared.

"He told me yesterday."

"What do you do?" She stepped closer.

"I own a diner. Doc Dennis never arrived for breakfast today." Charlie took a deep breath. Three steps down from the door of his diner to the sidewalk—a man with one leg would have trouble with those. "When you see him, you tell Doc Dennis that Charlie Harrigan will make sure he can get in. His breakfast is on me. Every day."

Homeless on Fisher Peak

Jan Verhoeff

Color drained from the sky, settling into the valley beyond Spanish Peaks in layers of coral, gold, and scarlet. As the lights twinkled to life across the land, darkness hovered close. Night sounds stirred restless from the heat of the day, and Jude War relaxed into a shelter of green canvas tarp and his sleeping bag, a haven from the night.

Promised twinkling stars danced high in the night skies, and randomly, as clouds drifted over, raindrops fell on parched dry land. Jude pulled the sleeping bag tight around his shoulders and held it close praying for relief. Relief from the relentless heat of the noon day sun, and of the night chills, and again of the night. Jude prayed he would find a place to settle. He wanted to get off the road and settle down.

He wanted a woman.

In the deep chill of the night, he dreamed of a flaxen hair, warm supple lips, and the light of the Lord in her eyes. He dreamed of a woman who would walk by his side and join him in his walk of life. He considered a moment, the kind of woman who would have him, as he awakened from the night. He longed for a woman to hold onto for all time.

Jude dreamed.

As the night birds sang their lilting song, Jude dreamt of a woman with warm brown eyes and skin, silky and smooth. Beside him, she warmed the night and stilled the fear of dawn. Jude fought to remain in his slumber, even as the light of day brightened his canvas cover, and rain splatted against the ground near him. Another rainy gray morning. He rolled up his sleeping bag after he'd fastened his clothing. He pulled his feet out one at a time and buckled on his shoes, boots that laced to the top with buckles that surrounded his ankles. Thick rubber soles provided comfort for his feet. He hovered under the tarp remaining dry in the storm until his pack was loaded and secured. He stood and buckled his pack on his shoulders, tightened it at the hip, and wiggled until it was comfortably in place.

With no wind blowing the slow drizzling rain was at least manageable. Jude hovered under the tarp, preparing the moment when he'd lift the poles and fasten them to the front of his pack. The back of the tarp would hang low, shielding his legs as he walked, and he'd remain mostly dry, walking away from the falling rain. Fortunately, what little wind there was blew from the north, and his voluminous cover would shield him from that.

He looked beyond the valley to the mountains and realized the fog hung low above him. He could readily see the foot hills, but snow covered peaks were out of his view.

He strolled thirty feet back to the east and walked along the railroad track, on dry rocky ground, one foot after the other, the miles passed.

He hadn't taken time for a meal, and hunger pangs met him as the first sign of clearing skies became visible to the south. In a lower pocket of his pack he carried meat sticks and a bottle of clear fresh water. The camel back was dry, and he only had two more bottles in his pack. He'd need to restock when he entered the next town.

A thought crossed his mind, "Is the next town where I'll stay?"

On the road for nearly seven months, he hadn't yet found a place where he wanted to remain, and hadn't thought he might... Until now. As he walked uphill into the edges of a community, he stopped to look around. No signs told him the name of the town. No houses welcomed him. No lights on porches revealed the pleasant warmth of families within. Instead, the town appeared abandoned, forlorn, and lonely. He looked at the few small structures he could see, and wondered if there were people here. He wondered if the town was bigger. Or was it just a wide holler?

Somewhere he heard a dog bark, and a mom telling her child to "get back inside, out of the rain."

A few yards further, he heard a door creaking in the wind, and realized the house near the edge of the road appeared to be abandoned. He looked around and stood quiet, waiting. He heard nothing at all. Silence appeared to mock him. He waited a moment longer before he strode past the open gate and up the steps to the wooden porch and entered the empty house. He ducked under the door with his tent cover, and pushed the door closed behind him. Inside, he carefully untied the cover, and removed his pack. The old house was dusty, but appeared to be safe, not too far gone, although the windows were broken, and glass scattered across the floor. Jude leaned his pack against a dry wall and hung his canvas tarp across two broken chairs to dry.

He wondered through the rooms and found an old broom leaning against the kitchen sink. He swept dust and broken glass into piles, revealing a sturdy wooden floor.

In the melancholy of a winter day, the home seemed dark and somewhat dingy, but as the sun sparkled through the boarded up windows late in the afternoon, he realized it wasn't dark at all. The walls were pale, gray stucco, and the wood still had a light sheen.

In a bedroom up the stairs, he found glass leaning against the back of a closet, and pondered how many windows he could fill. With the dirt and glass swept into piles, the floor looked less dangerous to walk. Jude used the dust from his piles, and threads from a tattered curtain with a little water from his bottle to make a paste to run around the edge of the glass in the three windows he could fill with glass.

One room would be warmer, with no wind whistling through between the boards.

Charlotte finished her work and gathered her belongings from the desk as the sun sank low in the western sky. She was leaving work early, but she'd arrived earlier than scheduled in the morning. She was done for the day.

Lingering clouds colored in pinks and orange as the sun descended in the horizon. Charlotte glanced at the massive bank of clouds and welcomed the next wave of rain and winter, as the sun dropped behind the warning. She drove across the valley and up the side of the mountain to her home, overlooking the lights of town. Before she arrived at her home, she remembered that she needed a few things from the market, and stopped to grab them from the closest store.

"Long night coming..." Carl, the clerk at Catty Corner spoke as she rushed inside. He talked as if they'd had a conversation going.

"It looks to be colder," Charlotte answered, grabbing milk, bread, butter, and eggs from the refrigerated section at the back of the store. She considered a bag of popcorn, but passed it by, since her hands were full. She placed her purchases on the counter and pulled a bill from her wallet. "Are you working all night?"

"I get off at midnight. Sonny is coming in, he's been on vacation, but I hear he's back and ready to work." Carl answered, ringing up her goods and bagging them as he went. "The last issue was a beauty!" He nodded at the community paper.

"Lots happening here this winter," Charlotte nodded. "I hope to publish a Christmas Edition this year, we have so much going on."

"You need another writer," Carl nodded, placing her last item in the bag.

"Maybe? Or a salesman, so I can write and he can sell ads," she lamented. "I'd rather write."

"That might happen." Carl handed her the change from her bill and offered to carry out her groceries.

"I got it," Charlotte smiled. "Thank you!"

She lifted the second bag off the counter and spun around so fast that she bumped into the stranger standing behind her.

"Oh, my!"

He caught her, one arm preventing her from falling and the other holding his own groceries from the store shelves. "Careful there!" He grinned.

Charlotte blushed, "I'm so sorry."

"No worries." He placed his groceries on the counter without letting go of her, then skillfully took her bags and carried them out to her car. "There you go!" He grinned, noting the continuing blush on her cheeks.

"You didn't have to do that," she smiled, looking up into dark eyes.

"No worries," he said. "It was my pleasure."

"Thank you." She nodded as she swung her feet into the car and he closed the door.

He nodded, as if he might have tipped his hat…

Had he been wearing one?

Charlotte considered the masculine aroma of pine and dust as she drove home. She pulled into the drive and parked under the carport, then carried her groceries in the back door. The cheery little house seemed brighter, a bit cozier when she turned the lights on.

She prepared a light meal of scrambled eggs and cheese, toast slathered with butter, and a tall glass of icy cold milk. When she finished, she placed her dishes in the dishwasher and pushed the button to start it. More often than not, she only ran it once a week, but she'd eaten at home every night this week, and it was more than half full.

The gentle sloshing sound lulled her back to the moment, when the stranger caught her in the store.

Nights on the mountain could be lonely. She let herself feel the soothing touch of his hand on her waist as he steadied her, and the smell of him. She remembered the smell of pine and dust.

A song came to mind and she began to hum the tune as she gathered a book, and the cozy comforter that she preferred when lounging on her couch. For a moment she considered remaining dressed, but that moment passed and she escaped to her room to find something more comfortable to wear.

A pair of light gray knit pajama bottoms, and a pink knit top that clung to her fully rounded figure, implying she was plump. She smoothed the fabric, and slipped her toes into the fuzzy pink mules she'd received in her Christmas package the last Christmas, before settling into the couch with her blanket and book.

Sleep might have found her for a bit, between pages of her book, before the knock came at the door. Charlotte pushed the book and blanket aside to walk across the room.

Outside, rain pelted the ground, and the sound of rushing water splattering on her porch greeted her as she opened the door.

"I just noticed as I was walking past that there's a light on in your…"

The voice was familiar.

"Come in!" She urged, realizing he was nearly standing under the fountain of water pouring from her drain spout.

"Oh, I?" He looked back, then stepped inside the door, pulling the storm door shut behind him. "I just stopped by to let you know there's a light on in your car."

"Oh?" Charlotte looked guiltily across the room. "I must not have gotten the door closed, when I came in earlier."

He nodded, "I can close it for you, if you'd like?" He offered.

"Oh, I can step out the side door…" She smiled back at him. "Come inside, you're practically drenched! Are you walking in this rain?"

"Just a bit further." He admitted, "I needed a few things from the store. I didn't realize when I knocked that it was your car…"

"Oh, I brought in the groceries, intending to go back and get my bag from work. But I got cozy instead." She nodded at the blanket and book, "Come in. I'll run close that door."

Before he could argue, she rushed off through the side door, and he heard the car door open and close. She returned momentarily with a shoulder sized tote filled with files, and paperwork, a computer, and several copies of the local newspaper.

"You should get out of those wet clothes. I can throw them in the drier for you? I have a…" She glanced at the closet behind the door. "I have some sweats you could put on, while they dry?" She pulled a bag of new dark blue sweat pants and a sweatshirt from the shelf.

"Oh, you don't need to bother… I'm okay. I'll have to go back out in a bit to get home…" he pointed out.

"The rain may stop?" She encouraged.

He took the sweats and walked down the hall to the bathroom where she pointed to a hot shower. He considered for only a moment, before he took advantage of the hot shower, to wash off the dust of his trail. Out of the shower, he dressed in the sweats, and carried the jeans, shirt, and heavy jacket to the laundry across the hall.

She dropped them in the washer, and grinned. "They'll be nice and clean as well as warm?"

Jude raised an eyebrow, watched the warm water hit the clothes in the washer, and realized he was going to be there for a while.

"Have you eaten dinner?" She asked, already working her way past him into the kitchen. "You must be starving, and cold. I put on a pot for tea, or I can make coffee?"

"Coffee? Oh, that does sound good…"

Jude tilted his head and watched her fill the pot with water, change the filter, add coffee, and set out two large cups. She filled one with cream, and offered him the carton of cream. He took the container and poured a few spoonfuls of cream into the cup.

"Jude War," he stuck out his hand, when she'd turned around from preparing the coffee.

"Oh, Charlotte." She grinned, "Charlotte Harris. My friends all call me Char."

Jude felt the silky warmth of her hand in his, and held on a bit longer than intended. "Char? What a beautiful name," he covered for the moment as he let go of her hand.

"Jude War?" She said his name, as if it were a question. "Are you from around here?"

"Not recently," he admitted. "I've been away for a while."

"Military?" She asked.

The tilt of her head indicated she'd recognized something.

"Bet you could tell by the high and tight?" He grinned. "Guilty as charged. Former. I just retired, 20 years in the Army. My last tour in Iraq."

"Retired, 44?" She guessed.

"45, but who's counting?" he asked, sipping the coffee she'd just poured.

"Age is irrelevant." She agreed, carrying her coffee and a plate of goodies she'd set out while they waited on the coffee to the dining room table.

Jude glanced around the room, noticing the wall of photos, including one in the center of her family. Charlotte was seated in a comfortable chair near the fire and there were three young girls around her chair, a baby boy in her lap, and three young couples surrounding her. Kneeling to one side was a young man.

"Your family?"

"My daughters and their husbands, my son, and grandchildren." She smiled, "They are scattered everywhere."

"They scatter fast, don't they?" He responded.

"Do you have a family, Jude?" She sipped her coffee and took a sliver of cheese, layered with a cracker and bit off a chunk.

"No. Military. I married early, but…" His voice trailed off, "She wasn't up to military life, and she left before we'd been married two years. Deployment costs a lot in the relationship realm."

"Sorry. I didn't mean to pry." She paused, "My husband died when Lex was two. I raised them, and all three girls are married. Lex lives in the city. He's going to college."

"Oh, still one at home?" He noted, realizing that's probably whose sweats he was wearing.

"In the summers. He works at the paper with me for a season, sometimes." She nodded, "He's won awards for his advertising work. He loves marketing."

"And you love to write?" Jude asked.

"Local stories. And books," she admitted.

He watched as she glanced across to the bookshelf and noted the matching covers stacked on one shelf. "Yours?"

"My latest, and the one above is Lex's book." She blushed, "His is better." She grinned proudly. "Mine is mostly fluff and purple prose."

"Nothing wrong with some fluff now and then…" He stood up and reached for one of each book. The cover of hers was a handful of purple flowers in a vase, with a clear bold title. Lex's book was dark, with a blue scaled dragon showing up in the darkness. Silver lettering made out the title and the authors name on the front cover. "Beautiful work."

"Thank you."

Jude settled into the chair and talked about various parts of the country. Eventually Charlotte changed the laundry from the washer to the drier, and returned to listen to Jude's stories.

With rain splashing against the windows, pounding the roof, time abandoned them.

The storm grew louder. They put their dishes in the kitchen sink and withdrew to the living room couch, to watch the weather channel. With a few ooohs and aaahhs over storm warnings, color changes on the radar, and jumps as thunder rumbled and rolled, they lingered until the power went out.

Safe and warm in the darkness, Charlotte curled comfortably into Jude's arm as the thunder rolled.

Time faded into the rushing waves of thundering crashes, light splintering the night skies, and waves of rain washing from the roof of her home.

Together they waited out the storm.

Not Even Solomon

Heidi Kortman

There! The goldfinch was going yellow again. His wavy flight path, with its rises and dips sketched freedom across the view through her patio door. Connie shifted her weight in the wide chair.

The slight movement made the old schnauzer snuggled in beside her lift his whiskered chin from her knee. Yawning, he stood, and dropped to the carpet. As usual, he stretched directly in front of her feet.

"You're going to have to move, beastie." She pushed herself upright before reaching for the purple paisley cane that leaned on the wall. Young Josh had used his birthday money to buy it, and she'd faked pleasure at the gift. The floral-inspired pattern was another painful reminder of what she couldn't yet do.

The dog shoved his nose into the corner of the door, and shook from head to tail. His tags jingled.

"You want out? So do I." Connie opened the patio door. The scent of damp earth floated in, accompanied by twittered birdsong, as the dog stepped through.

She pushed the sliding door farther open. If she kept a good grip on the door handle, she ought to be able to ease down sideways, so long as the rubber tip on the pesky cane didn't skid. No sooner had she planted the cane on the step than the telephone rang.

She lurched and caught her breath before pulling the cane inside again. "Hello?" Her voice was sharp enough to offend her own ears. Another breath, released slowly, settled her emotions somewhat. "Hello? Oh, Susan, it's you."

"Connie, I can tell you're not smiling. Look out the window. It's not sleeting today."

"I noticed, but what I also see is my rock garden. I can't wait to get my hands in the dirt, and my therapist says 'not for another month.' It'll be so overgrown by then,"

A cardinal called, and Connie leaned toward the open door to scan the upper branches of the oak just over the fence.

"Last Sunday, you told me you were making progress," Susan said.

"Not enough to suit me. I never realized how long this recovery would be, would seem."

"I've got an idea. Are you going to be home in a couple of hours?" Susan reached for some notepaper and tugged the cap off a pen.

"Yes, I'll be home all day. My next appointment isn't until Thursday."

"That's great. I'll be at your door at twelve-thirty. See you then."

The schnauzer put his damp paws on the step, and barked. Connie opened the door enough to let him in.

"Stay," she said.

Solomon waited on the towel--as he'd learned to do--until she'd wiped his muddy paws and rubbed his dripping whiskers. "You've had fun. I wonder what Susan is planning?"

The dog snorted and dashed the length of the family room and kitchen, where he jostled his food bowl against the wall. It clanged. He crunched kibble, then wandered to the sunny patch on the entry rug. Connie passed him, and pulled out the piano bench.

Afternoon sun lit the red and green sun catchers in the front windows as she played verses of a favorite hymn. Outside, the dogwood leaf buds had burst, and eventually, flowers would come. She struck a sour note. Her mind was back on gardening, and she couldn't kneel. Connie closed the lid on the piano keys and swiveled on the bench.

"Solomon, you don't belong in the living room." He'd snuck in behind her, and lay sphinx-like, to listen. "You always did like music."

Susan tugged the squeaky wagon down the path at the garden center. The Bleeding Heart bushes looked vigorous, and she hefted one with eight stalks of blooms into the wagon. Farther along, potted Lily of the Valley rhizomes lined a table. Susan paused. "Two, four, six, seven. That should do it." Humming, she chose the most burgeoning plants, and steered the wagon toward the bagged soil.

She rocked the wagon over an uneven paver. "Gotta renew my gym membership." Were the wagon axles going to support the load through the automatic door? Continuous squawks announced her progress toward the indoor cash register.

"Did you find everything you were looking for? Don't bother moving that bag of soil. I'll scan it from here." The clerk leaned over and aimed the scanning tool at the plump bag while Susan moved the remaining items to the conveyor.

"Jim will help you bring your purchases to your car."

Susan checked her watch. "That would be very helpful. Thank you."

She nodded to Jim, who hefted the soil bag into a different wagon and loaded the plants as the clerk rang up the total.

It took most of the gift card balance, and she was tempted to choose a new wind chime to zero it out, but to keep her word to Connie, Susan needed to leave. She led Jim to her van and opened the rear hatch. The bag stabilized the large planter already in the cargo area, and he stowed her plants neatly.

She started the engine and pulled out, accelerating toward the intersection, where the light hadn't yet turned amber.

"I'm through."

A police car left a side street ahead of her. Susan slowed. Three blocks later she turned down Connie's street and pulled up in her driveway. Susan phoned her friend.

"Hi, Connie, I'm here. Would you open your garage door and back door? I'll come in soon."

"Sure, just a minute."

Susan stepped out of the van and opened the hatch. She shifted the two-foot-tall planter from the corner toward the opening, eased it out, and dropped several folded newspaper sections into its mouth.

The garage door retracted. Susan walked to Connie's pegboard, where she grabbed a broad trowel and stuffed it between the newspapers in the pot. "Oof." Susan hefted the gift to her hip, carried it to the back door, and in.

Connie shut her refrigerator door and stared. "Where did you find that?"

"At an estate sale the day you were admitted for surgery." Susan shifted her grip on the burden. "Quick, take out the trowel and papers. If you'll spread the papers on the floor, I'll go bring in the rest."

Connie set to work, allowing Susan to ease the pot safely to the linoleum.

"It's not for strawberries," Connie said, "The openings on the sides are in the wrong position for that."

Glazed a rich green and carved with a pattern of long, tapering leaves, the columnar planter impressed even while empty. Six cup-shaped holes spiraled upwards.

Susan chuckled. "Keep guessing, I'll be back." On her way out, she propped the screen door open.

Solomon wandered into the kitchen as Susan returned, her arms full of Lily-of-the-Valley rhizomes. He circled, sniffing at the unexpected object in the middle of the floor, and pranced toward the door, greeting the visitor with his accustomed R-rr-r-r.

"Back up, old gray dog. These things are not for you. Go jump in your bed." Connie gestured, and the schnauzer obeyed.

Susan lined up the plants on the kitchen counter. "Now for the soil. The smallest bag I could find was twenty pounds." She wrestled the plastic sack into the house and propped it in the corner formed by the cabinets.

"More than we need for this, you're right, but you'll be repotting your African violets, so it won't go to waste."

Connie grabbed scissors from the tool drawer, and cut a corner from the bag large enough to admit the trowel. She moved a wooden stool to the paper-spread floor, settled, and scooped earth into the green pot. When the level reached the first cup, she took one of the rhizome pots from the counter, and set the contents in the cup.

"Thank you, Susan. It feels so good to have my hands in earth."

"When I saw the planter propped against a tree, I knew I had to make an offer on it. The estate sale had already run a full day, and this 'had your name on it' as we say." Susan lifted the next container from the countertop to hand to her friend.

Connie continued scooping, and filling the side openings. The last rhizomes went into the mouth of the antique. "It's too tall for a centerpiece on the kitchen table, but it'll be so fragrant I'd like to keep it indoors for a while."

"What if it stands on your hearth? You can have it brought out on the patio later."

Connie smiled and dusted off her hands. She stood, surveying her family room. "On the left side, I think. So pretty, and now we need to get it there. My little cart in the back closet should work." She retrieved and opened the cart.

Susan crouched and lifted the filled planter into the cargo crate. Connie gathered up the newspaper, trapping the spilled earth, which she poured back into the bag. The papers got stuffed into the trash before Connie pulled the cart to the hearth.

When Susan transferred the planter to the bricks, the sound brought Solomon into the room. He got his blue racquet ball from the behind the chair and bounced it on the carpet. Connie eased down onto the hearth beside the filled planter, and counted the stalks suspending buds of future flowers.

"In the next few days, this will be spectacular. Do you have time for a cup of tea?"

"Not today." Susan shook her head. "My daughter has an eye doctor appointment, and I need to meet the bus that's returning her to school after their field trip." She folded the small cart and trundled it toward the hall closet. "Can you believe Alyssa's eager to get new glasses? I wouldn't have been, at her age."

"You spent more time dangling from the playground monkey bars than you did reading."

"True." Susan chuckled and stepped out the back door. "Send me photos when it blooms."

"Too bad I can't also send you a whiff of the scent, as well."

The door closed behind Susan, and Solomon brought his ball to Connie's feet.

Competing for the Hearty Hearth

Mishael Witty

"What time is it?" Sadie Wright glanced up at the wooden clock emblazoned with the Louisa May Alcott quote: "She is too fond of books, and it has turned her brain."

9:47; 13 minutes before the Hearty Hearth Bookshop and Cafe opened. Giggie wasn't ever this late. She was usually here before 8:00, making sure there was hot coffee in the pot, food in the cat's dish, and welcoming incandescent light streaming down from above, illuminating the overflowing bookshelves Sadie had been in love with ever since she was a little girl. But Sadie had to complete all those tasks herself when she walked in the door at 9:15, and the gray-and-white striped store mascot, Mr. Browning, had let her know in no uncertain terms that he was not amused at having his breakfast served so late.

"Where is she, Brownie?" Sadie asked the cat as she set out some muffins on the granite countertop next to the carafe.

The cat responded with a disdainful meow and curled up in front of the fireplace.

Just as she set the last gigantic, fluffy chocolate chip muffin on the silver tray, the door jingled open, and her grandmother breezed in.

"Sadie, we have to talk, sweetheart."

"Giggie, we don't have time to talk now. The morning regulars will be in any minute."

Her grandmother cocked her head and gave her a quick look that said, "Why are you arguing with me, kid?" Then she shook her head and smiled. "We need to talk."

Sadie sighed. She recognized the tone in her grandmother's voice--and the look in her eyes. "What's going on?"

"This is my last day working at the store."

Sadie blinked, and the corners of her mouth turned down. "Excuse me?"

"I'm retiring. I've been at this way too long. It's high time I turned the reins over to you so I can spend some time traveling all over the country like I've always wanted to. I've got cousins I haven't seen in years, and your Uncle Ben has been at me for months to come to Georgia and see his peanut farm."

"Wait...What? And you just decided this, when? This morning?"

Giggie shook her head, and one silver curl fell down over her left eye. She pushed it back with a wave of her hand. "No, not this morning. Last night."

Sadie plopped down on the bar stool behind the counter. Good thing something was there to hold her body weight. "I don't understand. How long have you been planning this? And why didn't you talk to me about it?"

Her grandmother sighed. "Sadie, dear. My eightieth birthday is right around the corner. I've been thinking about and planning this for at least the past couple of decades. And I didn't talk to you about it before this because I knew you'd react this way."

"Well, how else am I supposed to react?" She was pouting. She took a deep breath. "I thought you loved this place." Nope, still pouting...and now whining too.

Giggie inclined her head forward and placed a steadying hand on Sadie's trembling arm. "I do love this place. And that's why I know I can leave it now. You love it every bit as much as I do, and you're going to do an amazing job of running it. I was a little worried at first, when you went off to college. I was afraid you were going to major in something useless, like English. But when you went after that business degree, I knew your head was in the right place. You were ready to pull up your big girl pants and get the job done. That's one of the things I've always admired about you, sweetheart -- that and your beautiful compassion for others."

Sadie grimaced, remembering all the hours she'd sat in finance and management lectures, wishing she could tear her ears off. At least someone was glad she'd steered away from English, and the knowledge she'd gained had helped her out tremendously when it came to dealing with the day-to-day store operations. She had to admit that much. Still...

"I can't do this alone," she whimpered, not so sure her big girl pants were in place. Tears threatened to well up in her eyes, but the jingling of the opening door forced her to blink them back and plaster as genuine a smile on her face as she possibly could as she went to greet her first morning customers.

"I don't have to do this alone!" Sadie leaned across the table at the local pizza parlor, where she was having dinner with her best friend, Marti Horine.

Her friend waved her plaid-clad arms in front of her chest in an apparent attempt to try to keep any of Sadie's words from sticking to her. "Don't look at me."

Sadie laughed. "No, I'm not talking about you. I know you have absolutely no interest in running a business of any kind."

Marti gave a quick nod. "That's right. I'm totally okay with my supporting role as the receptionist at the vet's office."

"But this idea has been running through my mind all day. I just can't get rid of it. The bookshop is too much for one person. That's why Giggie hired me straight out of college. She probably couldn't wait for me to graduate." Sadie sipped her soda pop through the bendy straw. "I need someone to help me run the bookstore."

"Don't look at me," Marti repeated.

"I'm not. I need someone who's fully committed to the store, just like Giggie knew I was. Am."

Her friend nodded. "Okay."

"So...." Sadie made a drumroll on the Formica tabletop with her hands. "I'm going to run an essay contest to find my next co-owner."

Marti spewed strawberry lemonade from her mouth and gasped. "You're what?"

"I'm going to run a contest for someone to become the next co-owner of the Hearty Hearth." She pulled her cell phone out of her pocket and checked the time. "I wonder if it's too late to call the newspaper and get a notice put into the morning edition."

"Considering the newspaper's editor-in-chief has had a crush on you since elementary school, I would think it would never be too late. He'd probably be thrilled to get a phone call from you at any hour of the day." Marti grinned and winked. "Or night."

Sadie wadded up a napkin and threw it across the table at her. She took a bite of her half-eaten pizza slice and set it back down on the plate, glancing around the room. Where was their server? "I've got to run. I still need to work up some sort of flyer to post around town tomorrow and maybe post some around the next town over too. And I need to write a blog post."

Marti held her right hand up in front of her face. "Say no more. You want me to get the check?"

She nodded her head so vigorously her glasses almost slid off her face. "Would you, please? I'll pick up the next one."

"No problem. What would you do without me?"

Sadie laughed. "I don't even want to think about it."

First morning light streamed in through the vertical blinds in the bookstore's back office. It was still difficult to think of it as her office, even a week after Giggie dropped the bombshell news about her retirement. Sadie shuffled the papers on her desk slightly and rubbed her tired eyes. These early morning hours were really starting to get on her nerves, and so were the hundreds of essay entries she had to read before she could find her new co-owner.

This was supposed to be a good way to find the perfect person for the job? Sadie groaned as she tossed yet another essay into the recycling bin. Not one of these was written by the person she was looking for. She glanced at the as-yet-to-be-read essays. Still plenty more to go through.

She took a deep breath and picked up another print out. Minutes later, after reading almost perfectly crafted prose presenting a community-focused message that brought tears to her eyes, she let the piece of paper drop to the desk in front of her.

"This is it!" A smile spread across her face, and she clapped her hands together in excitement. Her eyes darted to the top of the page. She'd purposely avoided looking at the name of the essay's author before she read it, just in case she knew the person who wrote it. She didn't want any personal feelings to cloud this very important business decision. But reading the name at the top of the page made her blood run cold: Jenna Rose.

"No!" Sadie cried and turned the paper over in her hand, as if that one simple action could erase the name that was on the other side, along with the brilliant essay written by the next co-owner of the Hearty Hearth. "No, no, no, no, no!"

But maybe it wasn't that Jenna Rose … the girl who'd threatened to punch her lights out if she didn't write all her high school papers. Surely it wasn't *that* Jenna Rose. It had to be some other Jenna Rose. That Jenna Rose wouldn't have written an essay like this. She couldn't write an essay like this.

She pulled her cell phone out of her pocket and furiously texted Marti's number. *I found the perfect essay.*

Her phone dinged to notify her of the reply a few seconds later. *That's great!*

Not so great.
Why not?
Winning essay was written by Jenna Rose.
Are you sure?

Was she sure? Well, no, not really. For all she knew, given Jenna's history, she could've had someone else write that essay for her and then turned it in as her own just to get half of a business. Her business. Sadie wasn't going to give that up to her. No way.

No, but her name was on it.
Wanna meet for dinner later?
YES!!!
OK. Come by around 7.
OK. I'll bring Chinese.

Sadie stuffed her phone in her pocket and turned back to the stack of papers looming in front of her. She doubted that any one of the other essays would even come close to being as perfect as the one she hoped hadn't really been written by Jenna Rose, but she had to try to find something as good. She just couldn't give this victory to her old enemy.

———•●•———

"I've got her phone number. I'm going to call her," Sadie said around a mouth full of eggroll.

Marti narrowed her eyes. "And what, exactly, do you think that will accomplish?"

She shrugged.

"It's not like she's just going to come out and say, 'Hey, you're right. I did have someone else write that essay for me. Here's the name of the person who should rightfully be the next co-owner of the Hearty Hearth.'"

"Well, at least maybe I could get her to admit she didn't actually write the essay."

"Again, what would that accomplish? You know she didn't write the thing herself."

Sadie frowned. "I don't know for sure."

Marti set down her chopsticks and stared at her. "How many of her own papers did she write in high school?"

Her shoulders slumped. "None."

"Um-hmm. And what in the world makes you think she wrote this essay by herself?"

Sadie shrugged. "I don't know. I just wanted to give her the benefit of the doubt."

"She's proved over and over again that she doesn't deserve the benefit of the doubt."

"Maybe. I still feel like I should talk to her. None of the other essays even came close to being as wonderful as hers… er, the one she sent in. I have to find out who wrote that essay."

Marti threw her hands up in the air. "Fine. Suit yourself. But I think you're getting ready to open up a big can of worms that's better left closed."

Sadie stood behind the bookstore's coffee counter and stared at the front door. It was still too early to expect customers, but she was expecting Jenna Rose to walk in through the door at any moment. She'd talked to her briefly on the phone last night after Marti left and asked her to come in to the store the next morning.

She yawned and poured herself another cup of coffee. She hadn't been able to sleep at all in anticipation of this morning's meeting. What was she going to say? How was she going to get Jenna to confess to what she'd done? And how was she going to get her spill the name of the real essay author?

She didn't have long to wonder. The door jangled open, and in breezed the one person Sadie had hoped she would never see again. Even after 10 years, the fear and anger mixed together in the pit of her stomach and made her queasy. Or was that the coffee? Maybe she should have eaten something before she downed that third cup.

"Sadie!" The word practically bubbled up out of Jenna's mouth. "Long time no see."

Not long enough. Sadie gritted her teeth. "Hello, Jenna. Thank you for coming."

"Is this about the essay contest?"

The hopeful look on her face was like a blowtorch to the ice block Sadie tried to form around her heart. She cleared her throat and nodded. "Yes, it is."

Jenna looked around the room to see if anyone else was in there watching them. Finally satisfied that they were alone, except for Mr. Browning, who was perched in his window sun spot, she said, "And?"

Was she serious? Sadie blinked. "And... You didn't write that essay, did you?" Way to just blurt it out. She bit down on her lower lip.

"What? Of course I did."

Unbelievable! She actually looked offended. "Prove it!"

Jenna shook her head as she took a step backwards toward the door. "I don't understand."

Sadie cocked her head. "What don't you understand?"

"Why do you think I didn't write that essay?"

A mirthless laugh escaped her lips. "Because you never wrote a single thing in high school. I wrote everything for you! Have you forgotten? Or are you hoping I forgot...because I haven't. I'm not anywhere close to forgetting that."

Jenna sighed. "Sadie..."

She shifted her weight to plant herself more firmly behind the counter and put her hands on her hips. "Prove it. If you want in to my business, you've got to show me you deserve it."

"Okay. How?"

"You wrote this on your home computer?"

Jenna nodded.

"I want to see it. And your email."

Her nemesis bristled slightly, but then her shoulders slumped. "All right. You win. When do you want to come over?"

Jenna's head was blocking the wall clock. Sadie pulled her phone out of her pocket and checked the time. Still another hour before the store officially opened. "How about right now? Let's go."

"I can't believe you still live in the same house you grew up in," Sadie commented as she studied the rows and rows of family photos along the walls. Some showed Jenna as a little girl, some showed her and her mother together, and some just showed Jenna's mother by herself. Almost all of the latter featured her wearing a bandana around her head, and she was lying in a hospital bed in some of them. She remembered Jenna's mom being sick for a long time ... around the time they were in high school.

Jenna shrugged. "After mom died, I inherited the house and never saw any reason to leave."

Sadie nodded, barely hearing the words coming out of her mouth. She was lost in her own memories. "Your mother, younger single mother, died--"

"Yeah." Jenna nodded. "My dad left when I was just a baby."

"And this happened right after high school."

"About six months or so after we graduated, yes."

Sadie slapped her hand to her forehead. "And she was really sick for a while before that."

She nodded again. "She was first diagnosed at the beginning of freshman year."

Sadie leaned forward slightly. "You weren't coercing me into writing those papers for you because you were lazy. You were worn out from taking care of your mom ... and probably grief-stricken."

Her grandmother's words of the week before floated back through her mind. *I've always admired your compassion.*

She saw the tears fill Jenna's eyes and felt her own eyes grow moist. "I'm sorry, Jenna. I didn't realize. I mean, I did…. But I didn't, really."

Jenna shook her head. "I meant what I wrote about the local bookstore being a lifeline for the community … showing people what the real meaning of community is. Your grandmother did that for me after Mom died. She led me to the perfect books and gave me an ear and a shoulder to cry on it whenever I needed it. And I would love the opportunity to help someone else the way she helped me."

Sadie laughed and wiped at her eyes. "I would love for you to have that too. You've earned it." She extended her hand. "Welcome to the Hearty Hearth, partner. We'd better get to work."

Bringing Granny Home
Heidi Kortman

"Terrific." Linda Arkin slammed down the phone receiver. The Evansville police had found Granny Alice seated at the kitchen table in her wedding gown and Grandpa Alvin's waders and phoned Linda's son. Trust her geriatric mother-in-law to foul up long-standing plans to shop in Kalamazoo. Joe was on his way to drive them south from Schoolcraft. Some other bargain hunter would go home with the Persian rug she'd had her eye on.

For the next five nightmarish days in her mother-in-law's disordered house, if Linda was lucky, she caught the tail ends of sly glances before the old woman slipped away to do mischief while Joe discarded trash. On the last morning, Alice wanted to walk around her neighborhood in her nightgown and Sunday hat. Joe managed to stop her on the front porch, but there she sat, obstinate. It took a solid hour before

Linda talked her back indoors, and into a suitable dress.

As Alice drank a mug of coffee with sugar and cream in the kitchen, Linda stopped her son in the hallway. She reached into her pocket. "Look! I've gone through her handbags, and I found cash. We'll need plenty as down payment for her room. We can't sell this house overnight."

"I found some too. When I kicked over a stack of books in a bedroom, twenty-dollar bills fell out. In all, I found nine hundred dollars up there," he said. "It's in my lunchbox. Want me to add what you've found to that?"

"Go ahead."

Linda yawned.

Something hit the kitchen floor.

"What stunt is she pulling now? Can't take my eyes off her for a minute."

Joe would rather have dental surgery than prepare to move Granny Alice's fish tank, but his son wanted the fish, so Joe'd take them home. He went to the basement and brought up a box of old canning jars. He dipped them one-by-one into the aquarium.

When each jar held water, he netted the agitated fish, and dropped them randomly into the jars. He'd already loaded the bed of his pickup with his lunchbox, a chair, a nightstand, framed pictures, Granny's clothes, and her television — and barely found room for the slimy tank.

"Ma," he yelled from the driveway, "Has Granny finished her coffee? I want to head home soon."

Linda came to the front door. "I'll get her." She turned aside. "Come on, Alice, we're going for a ride."

Joe wiped his hands and grimaced. He'd tossed thirty flowerpots full of dead plants into the Dumpster. Only a barrel cactus survived, squatting in its pot. The plant's four-inch spines would damage his new western boots, or he'd kick it. He eased it into the truck and slammed the tailgate.

His mother steered Granny Alice down the driveway by gripping the old woman's elbow. Joe opened the left door to the back seat of his extended cab pickup.

"Rides are exciting. Oh, look. Is someone moving?"

"Yes, Granny Alice. Let me help you in." Joe lifted her into the truck and secured her seatbelt.

As he fastened his own seatbelt, he glanced in the rear view mirror.

The old woman leaned as far as the belt would allow, her attention fixed on the jars of fish in a crate beside her. "One fish, two fish, red fish, blue fish. It's too tight."

Linda lunged for the canning jar and batted her mother-in-law's hands away from the lid. The old woman subsided into the corner and snuffled into a handkerchief.

By late afternoon, they'd traveled ninety flat Indiana miles. Joe pressed the accelerator harder. His pickup hit a seam in the pavement, and the barrel cactus jumped and rocked in the clay pot.

"I don't like this funny belt, Joey. I don't want to wear it. Where are we going?"

"We're going home, Granny Alice," he said. "Great Aunt Lola is there. You haven't seen her for a long time. You have to wear the seatbelt or I'll get a traffic ticket."

"Boy, do I want some uninterrupted sleep. I've had to keep an eye on Alice and her shenanigans every dratted minute." Linda yawned. "I never thought it would take me all week to find a home with an opening. There wasn't a single one in Evansville."

"It'll be okay, Ma. She'll fit right into that place where her sister is."

"I want a pickle. Where are we going? This isn't my neighborhood. I want to go home."

"We are going home, Alice. Are you hungry? We'll stop at that McDonald's," Linda said. She propelled the old woman to a seat in the corner of the nearest booth and sat at the edge while Joe placed their order.

"Mmmm, pickle." Granny Alice ate the burger and toyed with her fries.

Linda closed her eyes and rubbed her temples, until Joe yelped, "Ma!"

In that split second the old woman had painted the front of her dress with her ketchup-dipped fries. Fuming, Linda urged Granny Alice out of the booth. Ten minutes of wrestling behind locked restroom doors reduced the red mess to a damp pinkish spot on the yellow housedress.

Joe boosted the old woman into the truck. "We're going home. Won't you be glad to see Great Aunt Lola, Granny Alice?"

"Be quiet, Joe. I have a headache. I cannot believe it was that much work to take an old lady to McDonalds for a hamburger and fries." Linda Arkin glared at her mother-in-law, who plucked at the front of her housedress.

In South Bend, the biddy would be installed in a room across the hall from her sister Lola, and out of Linda's hair. She wasn't ready to tend the perverse crone, or face more meals like the one they'd finished.

"Oh Alvin, I made the loveliest dress. Linda, this dress is wet, and it's not pretty. Where's my pretty one?"

"The vintage clothing shop gave us a good price for it." Linda said, "And we need every penny."

The jars of guppies, neon tetras, and goldfish rattled.

"Ma, rearrange the towel in the crate," Joe said. "I don't want stinky fish water in my truck."

Linda twisted in her seat to grope at the towel that cushioned the jars.

"Did we go to the pond? What will Mother say when I bring home all her best canning jars filled with these funny fish?" Alice hummed, then started singing. "Down in the meadow in an itty-bitty pool...."

Linda twisted the radio knob. A distraction might keep her mother-in-law from opening those jars. Her search brought in a gospel station, and the strains of "Peace in the Valley" flowed through the cab. Linda looked over her shoulder. The old woman sat upright, with her hands folded in her lap.

"I've never gone to church in a truck before. No wiggling, Daddy doesn't like it! I know this song: 'There will be peace in the valley….'"

Linda heard her wobbly harmony, and drummed her fingers on the armrest. South Bend seemed forever away.

"I'll need to fill the gas tank, Ma." Joe's yawn exposed every tooth.

"Can't you stay awake long enough to drive straight through?" Linda said.

"Sorry, Ma, but I think I can make it to the north side of Indy. I hope the auctioneer gets good prices on the stuff from her house. My budget's tighter than ever." He rolled down the window for a blast of air, scented with drying hay. "You okay, Granny Alice?" When she didn't answer, he glanced in the rearview mirror. The old woman dozed.

Linda settled back. Granted, from the north side of Indianapolis it was a straight run to South Bend and the nursing home, but it meant a night of trying to control the impulsive woman in a motel.

Joe switched the radio station to one that played country songs, and lowered the volume to a murmur. Granny Alice snored in the back seat. Soon, one of his favorite goofy songs came on, and he lip-synced to the refrain.

Two miles from the exit for Interstate Highway 31 North, Granny Alice stirred in the back seat.

"Where is this? I'm hungry, and it's getting dark. Daddy says I have to be home for supper soon, but I don't see our barn."

Linda reached for her tote. She took out a notepad and pencil. "Alice, settle down. Draw me a picture." The tactic worked.

"There's a Speedway station ahead, Ma. I'll get some gas, and we can decide what to do about dinner, maybe find a motel." He slapped the steering wheel. "The rotten gougers raised their gas prices since yesterday."

"Use some of the money we found, son. After all, we're taking Granny Alice home."

He parked at the nearest pump. Then he shoved items around in the truck bed. Though he stabbed his arm on the cactus, he didn't stop until he could reach his lunchbox. He jammed one hundred dollars into the pocket of his jacket.

Before he paid for the gas, Joe stopped at his mother's window. "What do you want to do about supper?"

"I can't take Alice into another restaurant. Let's sign into the Motel 6. I'll get her settled, you go for pizza." Linda looked into the back seat. Her mother-in-law sketched with great concentration.

"Ma, we have rooms at ground level, fourteen and twenty. You and Granny Alice can have fourteen. I'll bring the pizza there. When Granny goes to bed, I'll go to my room."

"Come on, Alice, you can finish your drawing inside." Linda hustled her mother-in-law into the motel room.

Alice Arkin sat on the sagging chair clutching the note pad and pencil.

"You said we were going home. I didn't know you lived here. It doesn't look very nice."

"Granny Alice, this is a motel. We're staying here overnight."

"But I want to sleep in my bed, with my pillow."

"You can have the bed near the bathroom." Linda rummaged in her handbag for her migraine medicine, but found her tranquilizers first. She filled a glass.

"Here, take these vitamins." She held out the pills and the glass. "Take these, now."

Alice reached for the water. She sipped. "This tastes bad. I don't want it."

"Pizza Delivery." Joe opened the door. "I bought a large with ham and pineapple, and orange soda." He set the pizza on the dresser. Unlatching the lunch box, he dropped the change and his truck keys inside. "Enjoy this, Granny Alice. It's tastier than food at the nursing home."

Linda opened the sodas, while Joe lifted the lid of the pizza box and inhaled deeply. When Linda turned on the television, Alice chose a can of soda, dropping the pills into a different can. She resumed her drawings.

"The late news is over, Granny Alice. Time for bed. Tomorrow, you'll join Great Aunt Lola for lunch."

Alice Arkin finished her sketch and laid aside the pad and pencil. "Bye, Joey," she said as he opened the door.

"Good night, Granny Alice."

She lay still, rewarded with a penetrating snore from her daughter-in-law in the next bed. Alice dressed in the stained housedress and loafers. She undid the bolt on the door. Linda didn't stir, so Alice lifted the lunch box, and slipped out to the darkness.

"Vitamins, Alvin," she muttered, "Cullen's wife thought she'd lie to me. I know Valium when I see it. Nursing home, and lunch with Lola, not on your life. I haven't spoken to Lola in ten years. If she needs company, she can have her cactus back."

At the far side of the parking lot, Alice found a shopping cart. Then she used Joe's keys to open the truck cab. She dragged the canning jars into the cart. The lunchbox balanced on top. Panting, Alice wandered off.

Three hours later, farmer's market awnings shaded boxes of vegetables. Housewives and chefs haggled over fruit. Shoppers stepped aside for her cart. Vendors whose wares had sold packed up their stalls.

"My feet are tired, Alvin. Which way is home?"

"Hello, young lady. Why's a fine girl like you shopping alone? I have pickling cucumbers here."

The man seemed nice, with his tanned face and blue eyes surrounded by wrinkles from former smiles.

"I have the best pickle recipe, do you have dill?"

"Only the freshest," he said. "Come to the truck and I'll get it."

Alice paid with a twenty she pulled from the lunchbox. She couldn't wait to get to her kitchen. Alvin loved her pickles.

"I'm Alice Arkin. You remind me of my Alvin."

"My name's Bill Taggert. And you, young lady, are like my Hannah used to be."

Linda Arkin woke rested. She pushed her hair out of her eyes and saw the empty bed. Silence from the bathroom made her fling off the blankets, and listen at the door. "Granny Alice, are you in there? What are you doing, Alice?"

No one answered, and she opened the door. The room was vacant. Linda grabbed the telephone and woke Joe. "Granny Alice is gone. No, she isn't in the bathroom."

Joe arrived, shoving his flannel shirt into his jeans. "She can't go far. What's she wearing? Last time, she wandered in her nightgown."

Linda scanned the room. "She's in that dirty housedress, and her loafers. Joe, she's taken the lunchbox!"

"I put the truck keys in there last night. We're stuck until we find the old bat. Call the cops, Ma. We can't do this alone."

On the chair beside the cheap lamp lay her notepad—Linda flipped through the pages. "Oh Joe, look—I told her to draw pictures yesterday, but these are portraits. Here's your Grandpa Alvin and Granny Alice, and your father…look at his expression. She got it right. Here you are, and she drew me too. That ungrateful biddy…."

Linda cried, and Joe took the notebook. He tossed it on the rumpled bed. "Don't cry, Ma. That old woman doesn't know what she's doing."

"Them purty little fish'll be fine in the back of my truck, Miss Alice. I'll take all the corners slow. You ever make kraut? I've got some fine cabbages that will be ready in a week or two."

"I alternated taking pickles and sauerkraut to the fair, Bill, to let other ladies win. Peter Piper picked a peck of pickled peppers…"

Cactus Justice
an outtake from Wagon Train Orphan

By David Dockter

Wolf woke me with a low growl. I could hear voices down below. There were several men talking.

"This will be like taking candy from a baby," one said.

"There is only four of them, one's a kid and one's that girl. We've got them out numbered and this will be a good haul," another stated.

"I don't know Frank, the Indians seem to think that kid is something special," the first one spoke again.

"Don't be a worry wart. Here is what we'll do. We'll let them go for a couple of days and once they get relaxed on the trail we'll get them at night while they're sleeping. If they have a guard posted he will be the first to go. We leave no witnesses. That girl will be the last of them and the dead tell no tales."

A third voice said, "What about the kid's animals? That dog sure took care of that Navaho and they are saying that another one tried to steal that Black, and he killed him?"

"Like I said, don't worry a bullet will take care of the dog and if that horse proves to be too much trouble he will get one too," the first guy sounded a bit gruff.

"Okay Frank, we'll keep an eye on them and be ready to leave right after they do. There should be a bit of cash on them after selling them horses to the army. It will carry us to the gold fields." The second guy pushed for a plan.

Then it got quiet. I dared not move for ten minutes to make sure they were gone. I looked down through the slats on the second level of the livery stable and no one was around. So, I climbed down and went to find Jason.

Jason was my partner, the one member of the team that had been with me longest. I mostly called him my best friend.

Leaving the stable, I ran into the hostler coming down the street. He had been on an errand of some kind and had no idea who the men could be but told me that we had better keep an eye peeled.

"Wish there was some way to avoid that," I nodded. "But, if it comes down to it…"

"Maybe we can do something about it, Mike. If what I'm thinking works, it will teach them a lesson they'll never forget. First we need to get a lot more rope lets go back to the dry goods store and get some." The holster was the caretaker at the livery stable, and a good friend.

What he had in mind he wouldn't say, all he would say was that if this did not work we would have to kill them and even if it did we might have to kill some of them.

Next morning, Jason and I wandered around town and made sure to tell folks that the livery was starting to close in on us. We told them there was just too much traffic in and out, we need to get a goodnights sleep. So, we were moving out to camp tonight and leaving the next day for California.

We met Jerry and Heather, the other two members of our team, and outside the eating place we told them what was happening. We talked loud, laughing, chatting up our plan so others could hear that we would meet them tomorrow a mile outside of town to come when they were ready.

Now this might seem that we were lying to folks, but we wanted the thieves fooled and this seemed the best way to do it. We realized that at most this would only give us a day's head start. They would still be coming after us. Riding out of town about mid-morning a lot of people seemed to take notice.

We arrived at the meeting place and pretended to set up a camp just in case anyone was following us. It was a good thing we did because Jason went out about an hour later and found tracks where someone had ridden out and stopped and watched us for a while before riding back to town.

A little while later the army arrived with Jerry and Heather. They were both dressed in uniforms and looked like soldiers, sort of. Heather was all girl and it was a little bit hard to hide that fact. We hoped that people would think that it was just another patrol and had not looked too closely. The Army stayed with us for a couple of hours before they returned to the fort. The travel was comfortable and we didn't notice anyone following so I guess it worked. We rode on till well after dark and made a fireless camp for the night.

Taking out at dawn the next morning, we kept a close eye on our back trail. Stopping for a bite to eat at high noon, we saw the dust on our back trail and they seemed to be coming up fast.

Jason said, "Go on, I'll take a look and get back with you."

But we thought we'd probably need to find a good place to camp long before dark. Returning after a couple of hours, he said, "You were right Mike. There is eight of them and they are moving fast."

Taking the lead, the following morning he brought us out at a faster pace than we had been going. About mid-afternoon we came to a place surrounded by rocks except for the very front. It was like a natural fort with a spring in the middle, a perfect place to camp except for the prickly pear cactus growing across the entrance.

Then Jason explained his Idea. "We will set up camp inside the rocks and then we will move outside of them after dark."

Mike and I will go and get some more cacti and place it with the rest to make it a much larger patch. Then we will keep watch. There will be a rope hidden, when they try to come in we will pull it up and trip them in the dark. With any luck all of them will fall into the cactus. That will discourage them. If not we will have to start shooting.

Jason had gotten a worn-out buffalo hide from the Navaho and we used this hide to load more cacti on and drag it to the entrance. We created a patch about twelve feet long and ten feet wide. Then we strung a rope out a couple of feet in front of it and covered it with a little dirt so it wouldn't be noticeable. The cactus grew low to the ground. There was not going to be a moon tonight. So, chances were that it would not be seen before it was too late.

Our fort was about a hundred feet inside that gate and looked like there was only one entrance. Towards the back there was a gap wide enough for a man to get through with a little climbing. As we set up camp we used a fire ring that had seen many uses. A good campsite for one is also a good campsite for others and would be used by them.

After dark, we let the fire die out and made some false beds in order to make the thieves think we were asleep.

Jerry and Heather took the first watch while Jason and I got some sleep. I was not too worried that they could approach us without us knowing. Wolf would let me know. One of us was on each end of that rope hidden behind some rocks. Jason and Heather were on one side with me and Jerry on the other. Jerry woke me about one to take over and then all we could do was wait. I was thinking that I would look real foolish if the thieves failed to attack. I shouldn't have worried. They came a bit before daylight, trying to sneak up on us. Wolf gave me his low warning growl, but I would have heard them anyway. They weren't very quiet.

Things didn't go exactly as planned, but it worked. As the thieves got to the rope Jason and I pulled it and tripped six of them. They all fell face first into the cactus. All had their guns drawn and when the six hit they lost their guns. Screaming and hollering with the pain of them needles stuck all up and down their bodies. They were out of any fight. One of the guns went off and ricocheted off a rock hitting another one in the shoulder. That left only one and after looking down the barrel of four rifles he just gave up and dropped his guns.

Getting the six up out of the cactus I almost felt sorry for them, each one had to have several thousand spines sticking in him and they were all about three inches long. It was going to take a long time to pull them out and even longer for them to stop hurting.

"Which one of you is Frank?" I asked.

"Next time you plan something like this you remember what happened today. We should kill you and be done with it or maybe take your horses and boots and just leave you. Them spines will do it for us if you don't get them out. But we are not going to do that either. We will take your guns and after we leave your friend here," pointing to the one that had not been hurt, "can go and get some help for you. Maybe bring a wagon I don't think any of you will be able to ride for some time. Remember the wages of sin are death and just because someone is young that doesn't mean they are an easy target."

If looks could've killed I would've been dead. Frank was a tough man and even through his pain he looked at me with more hate than I'd ever seen.

"You should've killed me," He said. "I will be out in the gold fields and I'll find you sometime. You'll die!"

When he said that, I pushed him with my rifle and sat him back down on the cactus. "Not for a while you won't and if I ever see you on my trail again I'll shoot first and ask questions later. You've had fair warning!"

Then we gathered all of their guns and ammunition and rode away. That is how we defeated eight robbers and killers without firing a single round. I was happy about that and hoped we would not ever have to shoot anyone again, but sadly that was not to be.

To Fly A Balloon

Krystine Kercher

Best friends Gina Pawson and Anita Fuentes sat on the wraparound porch of the Fuentes' home, sipping tea and discussing their next sewing project. Both women worked full-time, but on their Saturdays, they liked to sew.

Their last project was memory quilts for the local nursing home. Before that, they sewed receiving blankets and fleece caps for the maternity ward at the hospital. They'd done so many sewing projects now for their community and for themselves that they were running out of new and interesting challenges.

"I want to do something really grand and amazing," Gina waved her hand in the direction of the mountains in the distance to indicate size and scope.

Anita nodded. "I know what you mean. But…what?"

"Maybe a huge flag for the high school?" Gina scrunched her nose. "You know, like the one they covered most of the field with during the Superbowl?"

Anita snorted. "Will the high school pay us? That material costs money, you know!"

"Maybe it wouldn't be too expensive? What are those huge flags made of?" Gina set down her tea and pulled out her phone. "Giant flags are made of...what?" she typed into the search bar.

"Aha—Nylon fabric." She flashed a grin at Anita who nodded and leaned back.

"And...how much is that fabric per foot? How large would it have to be?"

"I've found a store online that sells it for $5.45 a yard..."

By now Anita had pulled out her phone too. "The area of a football field is 57,600 square feet. Let's see... 57,600 times $5.45 divided by three is...YIKES! No way." She shook her head and showed Gina the huge number on the calculator app. "And that is just the fabric. We are not doing that."

"But the kids would love it! Maybe we could get a bulk discount?"

Anita laughed and shook her head. "How many times do you think they'd actually use that thing if we made it? Once? Maybe twice? Where would the school store it? How fast would it be ruined?"

Gina sighed and set her phone down. "You're right. It's too much money and expense for too little joy. We need a better project."

Several houses away, a small boy climbed to the top of a small slide with a packet tucked under his arm. Gina watched as he threw the packet up in the air and then slid down the slide. The packet filled with air and revealed a hot air balloon-shaped kite that floated briefly in the air before fluttering to the ground.

Gina looked over at Anita to see that she was also watching the boy. "You know what we could make?"

"A hot air balloon?" Anita chortled. "Girl, you really are nuts!"

Gina grinned and took another sip of tea.

"You really think we can do that?" Anita met her glance. "How are we going to sell it to the guys?"

Gina shrugged. "A toy for them that they can fly? Are you kidding? The only question they'll have is who gets to fly it first."

"Yeah, but won't someone need a license? If we make it, don't we get to fly it too? Where can we fly it?" The questions bubbled out of Anita one after the other.

Gina held up her hands. "Whoa there—first we need to find out what it takes to make a balloon. Then we'll need to gather the materials…"

Anita leaned in. "We might need a new machine."

"We might."

"When do we tell the guys?"

Gina grinned. "Not one moment before we have to."

"Are you game to fly it?" Anita leaned closer. "No way am I going to let Tomas have first dibs on this. It's *our* baby. We make it, we fly it FIRST."

"Yeah, they can have second dibs."

"So, what's our first step?"

"Have you ever been in the air in one before?"

Anita shook her head.

Gina nodded. "Me either. I think we find a place we can go up in a hot air balloon, and talk to the pilot. We need to find out who makes the balloons, and where we can buy a pattern."

Anita booked a flight for them via Groupon while Gina arranged a tour of the closest hot air balloon manufacturer. The flight was exhilarating, but the tour convinced them that they would never be able to construct an entire balloon from scratch.

"Miles of cord, a burner, propane tanks..." Gina checked off her list.

"Don't forget the basket," Anita added, "And flight lessons."

"And a pattern and set of instructions, and material for the envelope panels. This project is going to be expensive." Gina leaned back in her chair by Anita's kitchen table.

"But so worth it! So...when do we let the guys in on our big surprise?"

"Let's sew the envelope first. What colors should we choose?"

They liked the idea of alternating colors on the panels in dusty purple, rose, and gold. The material arrived two weeks later.

Assembling each panel was easy, but stitching them together at the gores and leaving a pocket for a cord to run through created a bigger challenge. The more panels were stitched together, the more unwieldy the project became.

They moved their efforts to a space they cleared in Gina's barn and set up Anita's new heavy duty sewing machine. Hours followed with pinning, unpinning, and re-pinning. In between, Gina managed and fed the pinned fabric into Anita's lap as she sewed for an hour before they switched places.

Finally all the seams were sewed and every last pin was out. They added the valve and the valve cord, and all the cords in the gores.

Gina and Anita spread the balloon envelope out and fussed and tugged at it until they had it hanging from the rafters of the barn so that one full side could be seen.

"It's time to tell the guys." Gina grinned and rubbed her hands together. "You have no idea how much trouble it has been, keeping Tomas out of the barn this long."

Anita nodded. "Try explaining to Coop where all that money is going and why without giving away what we've really done with it!"

Gina's eyes sparkled as she laughed. "We need to do this right. Let's have a cookout. I'll bring the steaks, you make the sides? Then we can all come back here for dessert and sell them on spending even more money."

"Wow. Just wow," Cooper exclaimed as he craned his neck, staring at the balloon envelope. "Where did that come from?"

Tomas shook his head. "So this is why you wouldn't let me in the barn? That is muy loco." He grabbed his wife around the waist and swung her around and kissed her.

Anita laughed at their antics before answering Cooper, "We sewed it. It's all ready to go. All it needs is a basket, burners, and some propane tanks."

"And pilots to fly it," Gina added. "But first the pilots have to take flying lessons."

Cooper swung around. "You want me to fly this thing? Where do I sign up?"

"Whoa, buddy," Gina grabbed him by the arm. "We sewed it, we'll fly it too. Not just you."

Cooper grinned. "Fine. Where do *we* sign up?"

Anita went over to the table she'd set up just for this moment, and turned on her laptop. "Gentlemen, if you'll just step right this way?"

As they finalized their arrangements, Tomas asked, "So...who gets to fly it first?"

A Man Full-Grown and His Donkey
Oris George

Supper was almost over. Dad savored the last bite of blueberry cobbler and laid his fork on the plate. He looked at me and said, "Son. There's a stray donkey in the pasture with yer donkey. First thing in the mornin' after breakfast, you'd best go run that donkey out on the county road. He'll find his way home, wherever that is."

I panicked!

I took a deep breath and swallowed a couple of times. My hands started to sweat. My heart tried to leap out of my chest. My voice squeaked as I said, "I bought him from Bert."

I held my breath and waited for Dad's reply. He took his time shaking out his napkin and slowly dabbed the left corner of his mouth. By now, I had to breathe, but was afraid to let my breath out because it would rush like a great blast of wind. Mom stopped eating. (The look on her brow indicated a severe storm was about to hit. She, along with my two small brothers, waited for Dad to explode.)

"Now let me git this straight," Dad said. "Ya bought that donkey from ol' Bert without askin' me. First off, you shoulda asked me. Secondly, what in Sam Hill did ya use fer money?"

"Bert only wanted ten dollars for the donkey. I had five dollars in quarters."

"Oris, five dollars in quarters don't make ten dollars."

"I know. I traded five of my 4-H hens for the rest and the donkey's name is Jim."

"You did what? Have you lost your mind?" Mom hit the table with her right fist, rattling every dish. She screeched. "For one thing, we don't need another donkey on this place! Those hens were your 4-H projects. Money's tight around here right now. We need all the eggs we can sell. What in the world were you thinking? As usual, you were **NOT** thinking!"

She looked at Dad and sighed, "I'm at my wits' end with this kid."

For once, my two younger brothers were quiet. Being quiet didn't keep them from looking *all smirky.* I was in trouble. They were enjoying every second of it.

"Son," Dad said, "Bert did some tradin' with Mel Anderson. That's how he happened ta have the donkey. That donkey bluffed out the Anderson kids. They can't ride him. They can't drive him. He kicks and bites and is all around a badly spoiled donkey."

I sat in my chair trying to think of something to say. My thinker failed me. My mouth was dry. My heart dropped clear to my toes. I knew I was dead. Dad finished what he had to say and waited for me to answer. I looked to Mom, hoping she'd come to my rescue. "You got yourself in this mess, now get yourself out of it," she said, her voice dripping icicles.

The palms of my hands sweated like they did in Sunday School when Miss Perkins asked for volunteers to read a verse from the Bible. What was I to do? I wanted desperately to keep Jim. I knew I had to come up with an iron-clad reason and quick.

Like the neon sign flashing in the window of Al's Barber Shop, an idea began to burn in my fuzzy brain.

"Dad. I've always wanted another donkey to drive with ol' Blue."

"Son, I just told ya, the Anderson kids couldn't do a thing with that donkey. What makes ya think you can?"

"I know I should've asked you first before I bought him. Everyone says you're the best hand with a mule in the whole county, and I knew you'd help me straighten him out. Then I'd have the best team of donkeys around." My heart was no longer beating. (The only reason I was still alive was my body didn't know my heart had stopped.) It was news to me that Jim had so many bad habits.

Dad glanced at mom, then across the table at my brothers. They were smiling from ear-to-ear like two impish elves, enjoying every second of my uneasiness. Dad looked me square in the eye. "Tomorrow mornin' ya bring them donkeys home. After I set the water on the hay, that Anderson donkey and me'll have ta educate ya."

"Thanks, Dad. I'll have 'em home early." I breathed a sigh of relief. (My heart started beating again. I began to think I'd live.)

Dad leaned back in his chair. From his left shirt pocket, he pulled a Bull Durham tobacco sack and rolled a cigarette. I thought I saw a hint of a twinkle in his eye when he looked across the table at mom. He scratched a match on the bottom of his chair. I watched as he lit a cigarette. All trace of what might have been a twinkle in his eye had vanished. Not breathing regularly, I was now seeing things that weren't there. It must have been my imagination. Dad pushed his squeaky old chair back from the table, got up, and went out on the back steps to enjoy his last smoke of the day. When the screen door shut, I started breathing again.

Ralphie, my smart-alecky middle brother said, "Boy, I thought you was really gonna catch it from Dad, and I'll bet you can't do a thing with that dumb donkey. I hope you have to sell him and Blue both."

Not to be out done by his partner in crime, my little brother Eddie asked Mom, "Why didn't Daddy get mad at Oris for buyin' another donkey? 'Specially without askin' first."

"That's enough, you two. It's not your affair. Put your dirty plates in the sink and be off with you."

I started to clear my dishes from the table. Mom motioned for me to sit in a chair.

"Why didn't you ask your father before going off half-cocked and buying that donkey?"

"I don't know. I guess I wasn't thinking."

"Well, if you don't know, who does? Young man, you'd better start thinking. Do you hear me?"

Dad hadn't told me to take Jim back. He was going to help me with him. Now, Mom got into the act. When she used that tone of voice, experience had taught me she was gearing up for a long lecture. No way, did I want to face her or her practical way of thinking.

For once in their lives, my two pesky brothers arrived when needed. Entering the kitchen, Ralphie said, "Mom, can we ride our bikes for a while?"

Mom looked at the kitchen clock and said, "No. It's time you got ready for bed." I knew she'd have her hands full for a few minutes. I took advantage of the situation and slipped out the kitchen door.

Dad, sitting on the porch steps finishing his cigarette, said, "Son, will ya shut the chicken house door. If we leave the door open and a skunk raids the chicken house, your Mom'll have my head and yours, too. When that's done, come back, and we'll have a talk."

A knot grew in the pit of my stomach. My imagination kicked into high gear. Had he changed his mind? Was he going to tell me Jim had to go?

I shut the chicken house door. My stomach was plain sick with worry. I plopped myself down by Dad and watched him take the last drag on what seemed to be the end of his fingers. Dad always got his money's worth out of a cigarette. He carefully set the very small cigarette butt on the step. With the heel of his left badly scuffed black boot, he ground it into a small spot of light gray ashes.

With a very dry mouth, and a knot in the pit of my stomach, I waited for him to say something. He wasn't one for rushing into anything. I wanted to get this talk behind me.

Any boy fit to own a donkey can ride, drive, and work his donkey. If he can't, he'd best git rid o' the critter, and git hisself a lamb." He added insult to injury by saying, "No boy worth his salt would let a donkey git the best of him, no matter how ornery the donkey or how many boys he had buffaloed. Are you man enough ta tackle that donkey in the mornin'?"

"Yes Sir," I answered.

Come morning, I was up and had most of my chores done before Dad came to the barn. I milked two cows to his one. (He wasn't keen on milking anyway.) Dad fed the cows and calves. I swept the barn floor and fed the pigs and was ready to go to breakfast. But 'no-o-o'. Dad had to stop and check Mom's garden. (As if it wouldn't be there after breakfast.)

Halfway through breakfast, Ralphie piped up, "Daddy are you gonna make Oris take that donkey back?"

I wanted to punch him a good one. However, from experience, I knew hitting my brother wasn't the thing to do, especially at the table. The look on my face told the little twerp he was in for it the first time I caught him out of Mom's sight.

After breakfast, Dad shouldered his shovel and walked up the ditch to change the water. Hotfooting it over to the pasture, I caught Blue and tied her to the fence. With halter in hand, I walked up to Jim. He stood still as honey in a glass jar. He put his nose into the noseband, and I fastened the halter. "Heck fire, no trouble here," I thought. "This donkey's gonna be okay."

Blue was a good traveler. She walked fast for a donkey and Jim kept pace with her. All the way home, he didn't let the lead rope tighten. He let me catch him without any problem, and he led better than most horses. I was beginning to think that maybe Mr. Anderson was wrong about him.

As we turned into the driveway, one of my brothers threw a handful of gravel at Jim's feet. Blue shied away from the gravel intended for Jim. The gravel didn't bother Jim. Dad was still setting the water on the hay, so I turned Blue and Jim loose in the corral.

Over an hour passed. Dad still hadn't come to the house. Patience not being one of my virtues, I went back to the corral to issue to Jim his proper call as a beast of burden. With bridle in hand, I put my arm around his neck. He stood calm and peaceful as apple pie on Sunday. I tried to put the bit in his mouth. He didn't want any part of that foolishness. He clamped his teeth together like a four-inch vice. No amount of prying or forcing succeeded in getting the bit into his mouth. All at once, he turned into a hurricane of hair, mouth, long ears and feet that twisted-turned-jumped and bucked, trying to dislodge me and the hated bridle.

He stopped, turned in a tight circle and whopped me in the chest with his head. The breath blew out of me. I lay on my back in the dust and looked up to see him coming at me with all the furor of an Arkansas tornado, his mouth wide open, his ears laid back along his neck, and his eyes sparking fire. I rolled under the bottom pole of the corral as he came to a sliding, dusty halt. He stared at me through the poles of the corral with the most 'un-adult-er-ated' hatred I'd ever seen in any eye.

I was so mad I could 'spit' (and I did). I stood up, dusted off my shirt and Levis and crawled through the rails back into the corral. That durn donkey stood on the far side of the corral, head lowered, looking at some imaginary mouthful of grass. I approached him with caution. He raised his head. Faking innocence, he looked at me with big brown eyes as if to say, "Well, little boy, how are you this fine day?"

Jim surprised me. He lowered his head and took the bit like it was no big deal. The next step was to harness him. He followed like a lamb as I led him to the barn and tied him to the hitch ring by the door. I came out the door with a harness over my right shoulder. He turned his rump to me and started kicking like all-get-out. It was plain to see he didn't want any part of that harness. To make matters worse, trying to get away from that durn kicking donkey, I tripped over my own feet ending up on the dusty ground tangled in the harness. Hearing a chuckle, I looked up from my undignified position to see Dad sitting on the top rail of the corral (and to see that darn donkey grinning from ear-to-ear).

"Well, boy, are ya gonna put the harness on that donkey or hav' ya decided to wear it yerself?" he asked.

That did it! Upon removing myself from the tangle of straps, I brushed the dust off my shirt, walked over to Jim, and kicked him a good one right in the ribs. He kicked at me! I kicked him again. He kicked at me. I kicked him. His next kick caught me right in the gut, sending me rolling into a corral post.

"Don't let that donkey git the best of ya," Dad said. "Keep away from his hind feet! Could be he don't like the way ya comb yer hair or somethin'."

These were words that drifted down to me as I lay in the dust gasping for air. In my awkward position, I didn't appreciate the advice Dad was offering. My legs were shaking. I stood up and brushed the dust from my shirt and leaned against the post to catch my breath.

"Are ya OK?" Dad asked from his perch.

Of course, I was OK! After three more tries, Jim stopped bucking and kicking, and let me put the harness on him. By then, I was one worn out thirteen-year-old boy.

Dad said, "Leave the harness on that rascal and tie him ta the hitch ring. That way he can contemplate the events of the mornin' while we go up ta the house for a cold drink of water. It sure did make me tired and thirsty watchin' you and that donkey jiggin' around."

Every day for three days, Jim and I battled it out. No way did he want to be a self-respecting donkey and wear a harness. He didn't like the bit. He didn't like the collar. He darn sure didn't like the harness.

Late Saturday afternoon, Dad stopped to check and see how things were going. He said, "Are ya spendin' most of the time lyin' in the dust?' Yer mother tells me every time she looks out the kitchen window you're lyin' on the ground or brushin' dust off yer shirt and jeans."

One Friday morning, with bridle in hand, I approached Jim prepared to do battle. Something was wrong. He didn't fight the bridle and stood calm as peaches and cream while I tied him to the hitch rail. With caution, I placed the harness on his back. No trouble here. He stood calm and quiet. At last, my persistence had paid off. I felt like a man full-grown. I'd stayed with it and hadn't let that blue roan donkey bluff me like he had the Anderson kids. I patted him on the neck. I thought, "You ol' rascal. You ain't as tuff as you thought you were."

Wanting to show off a little, I went looking for Dad. He was in the shop putting new sections in the mower knife. "Dad, that ol' donkey isn't so tuff after all. He's standing at the hitch ring harnessed and ready to be hooked to the cart." Dad laid the ball-peen hammer on the work bench. As he turned to face me, I thought I saw the trace of a smile on his face. (It must have been my imagination.)

"Let's go have a look at 'im," Dad said.

"Jim took the bit and stood still while I harnessed him. He finally decided he couldn't get the best of me," I said.

Dad stood by the gate and looked at Jim. "From the way he's standing there, hip-shot, ears drooping, and eyes half shut, he don't seem much worried 'bout a thing," Dad mumbled. "Well, son, you gonna stand there all day and admire that donkey instead o' hitchin' him ta the cart? Should we take the harness off that donkey and go fishin'?"

"Let's go fishing," I said.

No argument there. I liked to fish as well as any boy in two counties. I'd been wanting to go fishing ever since school let out for the summer. However, Dad always found something that needed to be done. Every time I asked him if I could go fishing, he'd always say, "When we git work caught up."

"Reckon we could ride them donkeys over ta the fishin' hole?" Dad asked.

Dad smiled and said, "You git Blue and I'll git poles. Days like this are made fer breathin' God's fresh air and fishin'."

Grandad, with a shovel over his shoulder, stopped to see how things were going with Jim and me. "Seems like you and that donkey are no longer havin' a permanent disagreement over what is expected of 'im. Gittin' that donkey ta do what ya wanted 'im ta do seemed to be as hard as sneakin' a sunrise past a rooster," Grandad said.

"But remember this, patience is the price of survival."

"Son. Will it be okay with you if I ride Jim and you ride Blue?" Dad asked.

"Fine with me."

Dad went to the shop to get the fishing poles. I grabbed a shovel and headed for the garden to dig some worms.

By the time I got back to the barn with the worms, Dad had bridled Blue and Jim. "That donkey couldn't 'ave behaved any better," he said. "He took the bit like it was the thing ta do, no fuss at all."

After inspecting the worms and commenting on how any self-respecting fish couldn't possibly pass up such a tasty morsel, he handed me my fishing pole and told me to go ahead on and open the gate.

I felt like giving Jim a whack with my pole. After all the trouble I'd been having with him, with Dad, he behaved as calm as Mom's pet yellow cat. I was beginning to think that dumb donkey was just trying to make me look bad.

Aggravated as I was with Jim, I laughed when Dad came riding through the gate. I'd never seen him on a donkey. There he was brown Stetson hat set firm and proper, long legs which took the soles of his scuffed black boots to within inches of the ground, holding a fishing pole in one hand, and guiding Jim with the other.

"Whatcha laughin' at?" he quipped, as he rode through the gate with the exaggerated air of someone of great importance. "Leave the gate open. Yer Mom'll be home soon. She won't have ta git out of the car ta open the gate. Nothin' makes a woman madder than having ta open a gate, 'specially, if the menfolks have gone fishin'. I don't know what it is women have against fishin'."

"Hey men!" Grandad hailed. "How come it is I have ta tend this water while you two goof off?"

"Because we're better lookin'." Dad hollered back.

Grandad walked over to the fence. "Well, boy, how goes the donkey business?"

"OK," I said. "We're goin' fishin'."

"I'm glad ya told me," he said. "Otherwise, I'da thought you was just takin' those fishin' poles fer a ride."

Dad and Grandad discussed the hot weather, how it seemed early for it to be so hot and dry. They hoped there would be enough irrigation water for the rest of the summer. Grandad told us he and Elmer reached an agreement just a little while ago on who would use the water and when. If Elmer so much as tampered with the head gate while Grandad used the water, he'd find his hair parted with Grandad's #2 irrigating shovel. Dad thought that should be easy enough for Elmer to understand.

On arriving at the creek, Dad said, "Make sure Jim's tied ta where he can't git loose. I darn sure don't wanna walk home havin' ta carry all them fish we'll catch." Past experience had proven to me Dad would catch the most fish, and I'd end up carrying them home.

Dad had his special way of fishing. It was a ritual that had been handed down to him from his father. First thing, he would check to see at which angle the shadows of the trees were falling. Then, he would find a magic spot on the bank to set the can of worms. Many times, he had instructed me in the art of placing the worm can. If the can were too close to the bank, the fish would jump out of the water to get at the worms. (Of course, there would be no sport in that.) Next, he positioned his hat on the back of his head. It took several tries before the hat was just right. (Heaven forbid if the brim should shade his face!) Trout could see his eyes in the shade of his hat brim and then escape to the deep, black recesses of the fishin' hole. He'd sit on the ground 'just the right distance' from the can of worms and roll a cigarette. The last, and final part of the time-honored ritual before putting the worm on the hook, was to place the freshly rolled cigarette in the left corner of his mouth. Holding the fish hook exactly six inches from his mouth, he'd spit on the hook and light the cigarette. All this preparation would be to no avail if the fat, red worm wasn't placed on the hook head end first.

The long hot summer afternoon stretched out before us, a time of lazy, effortless fishing.

For the rest of my life, I would remember that gentle afternoon in the summer of 1946. When Dad started to talk, even the rocks and trees stopped to listen. He referred to times like this as quality time. He talked to me about always being honest in everything I did during my life, look for an honest cause to champion and give it my best, let people know where I stand on every issue, be it good or bad, always be respectful and kind to older people and those younger than me (even my two brothers), for an honest dollar, do an honest day's work, to believe in God and Country, realize every man can't be a poet no more'n a sheep can be a donkey, always remember the only thing gossip can't hurt is live sheep or dead people, pay attention to my own business, take care of my own problems, remember, all people, no matter the color of their skin or their station in life, are the same under the skin in every important way. They desire to eat, to sleep, to be dry and warm and safe against the coming day.

I caught a big fat trout. Dad caught a bigger one. I caught three medium-sized ones. His were always bigger than anything I could catch. My complaining brought a smile to his brown, wrinkled face. "Ya ain't holdin' yer mouth right or somethin'," he said. "Takes time ta learn how ta catch them r-e-a-l-l-y big ones."

"I'm learning," I said. Ring gave me a warm, wet lick on the left side of my face.

"Well son, it's gittin' late. It'll soon be chore time. Let's git on them donkeys and head fer home," he said. "From the looks of the clouds playin' 'round the tops of the Twin Mountains, we just might git a shower."

Blue and Jim headed home, their hooves disturbing the dust on the quiet road. A soft breeze from the west carried a fragrance of dampened dust on rain-struck grass.

It was the smell of a country childhood.

Apple River Bride

Lisa M. Prysock

I dedicate this story to Saima and her family, displaced Christian refugees from Pakistan who fled the sword to keep their faith in Jesus. Where they currently reside, they are unable to work or send their children to school. They seek a home in the U.S.A. for their family of 7. I'm praying for a miracle for your family, Saima. I pray for strength and divine intervention as you seek a sponsor to be able to come to America.

The setting of this story is Apple River, Wisconsin, in Polk County, where I went to kindergarten and remember writing my first story with the help of my teacher, Miss Landry.

Ellie stood back to survey the work her fiancé had accomplished on the log cabin since yesterday's visit. Today, the windows were visible. They didn't have glass panes yet, but she could easily imagine them from her vantage point. She stood on a clearing of gently sloping green lawn on a few acres her future father-in-law had set aside from his dairy farm for the young couple. Spring had arrived and it wouldn't be long before the cabin was finished. Each day, she brought Caleb lunch. If he wasn't busy, he'd stop working and sit down on a quilt and share the meal with her. If he was very busy, he'd give her a quick kiss on the cheek and chat for a few minutes—always with an explanation if he couldn't eat with her.

He finally emerged onto the covered front porch and strode across the lawn to her side when he'd peeked through one of the windows and noticed she'd arrived. "Hello my love." He pulled her into his arms and swung her around until she giggled with delight.

"Stop, Caleb!" she laughed, not meaning a word of it.

He stopped swinging her around and planted her feet on the ground, but he kept his arms around her waist and gave her a kiss on the forehead. "Mmm, you smell like gardenia."

"Do you like it?" she asked, hoping he would. It was her first purchase of real perfume. Mother had said she should have something now that she'd be married soon.

"I do," he nodded, his blue eyes looking attentive beneath his golden hair.

"We've got windows now," she smiled, changing the subject and drawing away from him a little lest his brothers find her in his arms. She didn't see or hear them inside the cabin today, but that didn't mean one or more of his three brothers weren't around somewhere close by. Not that they hadn't discovered them kissing before, but she didn't want to let it happen too frequently before they were officially wed. His two older married brothers—Joshua and Samuel—they wouldn't say anything, but his younger brother, James, would tease him about waiting and threaten to tell if it suited his mood.

"It's really starting to look like a home, isn't it?" Caleb asked, standing back to admire the view.

"It is." She nodded and searched his face, anxious to know if today she could stay and share the meal with him. Of course, she couldn't tell what he might say. Ellie could stay a while to observe either way, but Mama would wonder if she was gone longer than an hour. There was still much to do at home to prepare for the wedding.

"So, what'd you bring us for lunch today? I'm starved."

"Does this mean you have time for us to eat together?"

"Yes. My brothers won't be able to help until later this afternoon, so we can eat without being rushed."

Ellie smiled wide and reached for the quilt she'd placed at the foot of the tree when she'd first arrived. She handed it to him to spread on the blades of fescue stretching toward the sunlight. "Cold fried chicken, biscuits, potato salad, spring peas, and cherry pie."

"Cherry pie, my favorite! Keep feeding me like this and I'll have to marry you, Elizabeth Jean Calhoun," he teased, winking at her as he spread the quilt.

Soon they were seated beside each other sharing the meal, enjoying a quiet moment together. After a while, she blushed, realizing Caleb was staring at her with a dreamy look in his eyes.

"What?" she asked.

"Oh, it's just, I'm the most blessed man on the earth getting to marry you in a few weeks." He reached across the quilt and brushed a stray curl away from her green eyes. "The way the sunshine dances on your golden-brown hair and how your eyes sparkle with joy; it makes me happy knowing we'll soon be together forever. I'll be married to the prettiest bride in all of Wisconsin!"

"Oh, Caleb, I can hardly wait!" she replied, her heart beating rapidly to hear his sweet words.

The next three days, however, were quite different. Two of Caleb's brothers were there the first day and they were in a hurry to return to their regular farm duties. Pa Andrews, Mr. Marcus Andrews to Apple River residents, had said they were falling behind. The second day, all three of his brothers were installing the wood floor. On the third day, none of the brothers were around, but Caleb was quiet and seemed troubled.

"Is everything all right?" Ellie asked when she arrived and nearly collided with him as he exited the cabin and threw a plank of lumber on a pile of similarly discarded pieces where it landed with a loud thud.

"Just havin' a rough day is all," he replied, avoiding her eyes. "And please don't ask if we're going to have time for lunch because I don't. I hope you won't mind, but if you'd just leave the lunch on the porch, I'll get to it eventually."

Ellie, stung by his curt remarks, bit her bottom lip as he disappeared around the corner and inside the cabin, leaving her alone on the front porch. She paced the length of the porch and for about a minute, all the two of them could hear were her low-heeled boots clicking on the shiny new boards or his hammer pounding away. She hated seeing him this way, but maybe it was the pressure to keep up with his fair share of the chores around the farm and finish the cabin before the wedding so they'd have a place to live.

She finally stopped pacing, turned around, and ducked inside the cabin, giving her fiancé the benefit of the doubt. "The floor is coming along nicely."

The remark was her effort at keeping him cheerful, but he continued hammering in a corner where the floor wasn't finished. He pounded three or four times and then paused to reply. "Thanks. It's almost done and then we'll be able to frame in some interior walls."

She walked around on the floor, admiring more of the shiny new boards they'd picked up in a wagon load from the lumber mill in town. The exterior logs had all been cut down from the woods in various places on the Andrews' property.

Finally, he stopped hammering again. "I really wish I had more time to catch you up on everything that's been happening, but I promise we'll talk more in a day or two when I can take a break. I have to finish this floor by tomorrow or we'll be behind schedule."

She bit her lower lip again and quietly replied, "All right, Caleb. I understand. I have a lot of work to do at home to prepare for the wedding, so I'll just leave the lunch on the porch and we'll talk as soon as possible."

"Thanks, Ellie." He winked at her and went back to pounding nails into the boards as she turned to begin the twenty minute walk home toward the Calhoun homestead.

By the time she'd traversed half the way along the dirt road connecting their farms, she wondered if she'd be able to handle being married. What if they argued frequently? What if she wasn't able to keep up with scrubbing the floors, cooking, baking, canning, and washing? What if she didn't fit in with the wives of his older brothers?

What if she decided she wanted to become a teacher or a seamstress? What if she might want to write books? Would Caleb give her the wings to fly he'd always promised? What if he was temperamental or if they simply weren't happy after they married?

Deep down, she didn't think her Caleb Joseph Andrews, the third son of fine, upstanding neighbors such as Marcus and Jane Andrews, capable of causing her to become permanently unhappy, but she told herself any bride-to-be should at least consider the nature and character of a future husband along with the possibilities and ramifications of marriage. She picked up her burgundy skirt and white petticoats, cautiously navigating around a mud puddle. Then she continued along her journey, contemplating such complicated matters, unable to appreciate the delicate flower blossoms pushing up from the earth along the patch of trees to her right or the sparrows chirping from the branches above.

She was quiet when Mama made her stand still near the table in the main room and try on her wedding dress while she pinned the hem of the gown and fussed over the side seams.

"Hold your arms down at your sides now," Mama directed as her younger sisters, Mary Josephine and Anne Marie, stood back and admired the gown. Even Grandma stopped mixing up a cake batter in the kitchen to behold her granddaughter.

"Oh, Ellie, you look beautiful!" Mary Jo breathed as she held the pin cushion for Mama.

"Heavenly!" Anne Marie agreed, releasing a sigh and then dancing about the room humming the traditional bridal march.

"My, she looks like you did at her age, Louisa." Grandma smiled from near the doorway to the kitchen and blinked, appearing as though she was somewhere else in time. Ellie imagined she was remembering a similar moment two decades prior.

"Ouch! Careful, Mama!" Ellie jumped when one of the pins stabbed her rib cage, pricking her skin clean through her corset.

"Sorry, dear." Mama kept pinning and tucking as quickly as possible. "Turn this way. No, never mind. I'll just move around you. Remain still."

"You'll be the prettiest bride Apple River's ever had in this fine white satin. It shimmers when you're standing still." Mary Jo couldn't take her eyes off Ellie's gown. "Look at the fine beading, too. Mama, I think you've outdone yourself. Your gown will be the talk of the town for years to come. Just look at this bustle!" Mary Jo stood back to admire her sister in the bridal gown, both hands on her hips.

Her sister's reaction coaxed a wide smile from Ellie for the first time that afternoon.

"Mary Jo, bring the mirror from my bedroom so she can see it," Mama instructed.

"I really like the square neckline. It suits Ellie's figure." Grandma nodded approvingly, seeming to snap back into the present as if she saw her for the first time.

"Be a help, Anne." Mama spoke again through two pins she held in her lips, pressed together. "Bring me the lace over there on the parlor bench for the veil. Let's see how it looks on our Ellie. Elizabeth Jean, hold still."

When her sisters had finished helping mother position the veil, Mary Jo placed Mama's full-length oval mirror so Ellie could see the nearly completed gown for the first time.

For the second time that day, tears brimmed in Ellie's eyes when she turned to her side to see the puffy billows of satin cascading into a three-foot train—only this time, they were happy tears. "Oh, Mama, this gown is everything I dreamt it would be and more." Her hands flew to cover her mouth in joy and surprise that her mother had been able to produce the gown from the one Ellie had shown her from among the wedding fashions presented in Godey's Lady's Book. Whatever qualms she'd had on the walk home seemed to vanish as she realized their wedding day drew near.

"Caleb's absolutely going to be enraptured!" Anne Marie leaned forward with her elbows on the table and sighed, completely amazed.

"Will you have enough time to finish our dresses, Mama?"

"Not if I don't finish this gown by tomorrow." Louisa Calhoun stood back to survey her work with one finger propped under her jaw and an arm folded across her short-waisted torso. "So you girls best be a help to your grandmother with the chores for the next two weeks or no new bridesmaid dresses."

Her sisters glanced wistfully at the pile of pieces of fabric their mother had carefully cut from the violet satin for their dresses.

"Yes ma'am. We'll be a big help. We promise." Mary Jo spoke on behalf of both sisters.

"Let's set the table for dinner," Anne Marie suggested eagerly.

After dinner when the dishes had been washed, the family gathered around the main room near the fireplace. Mary Jo and Anne Marie studied their books for school. Ordinarily, Mama sat on the parlor bench beside Father. However, Mama sat near the kerosene lamp at the table across from the girls, stitching the hem of Ellie's wedding gown while Father read the newspaper from the parlor bench, pausing to add an occasional log to stoke the fire. Seated in a rocking chair beside her grandmother's rocker, Ellie's apprehensions only seemed to return as she rocked and silently pondered over her concerns. She kept her head down as she stitched what would become a set of crisp white linen curtains to match the blue and white checked tablecloth she'd made for her hope chest.

"Wisconsin is leading the nation in cheese production," Shane Calhoun announced as he shook out the newspaper to turn to a new article. "You might mention that to Marcus Andrews when you next see him, Elizabeth."

"Yes, father," Ellie nodded without looking up from her stitching.

"What's troublin' ye, Miss Ellie?" Grandma asked, the sound of her rocking chair creaking steadily on the wood floor. "You're awfully quiet this evening."

"Oh, am I? I'm just concentrating on these curtains to be sure I get the hem straight."

"Did you iron and pin the hem first?"

"Yes, of course," Ellie glanced up at her grandmother and did her best to refrain from rolling her eyes in exasperation. She had ironed the hem and pinned it, but she wasn't about to discuss the first crisis she had about marrying Caleb with the whole family present. Besides, she wasn't ready to share her thoughts — and because they were complex and varied — maybe not ever. Sometimes Frances-Jean Elizabeth Carter could be unsettling the way she always seemed to be in the know. Ellie bent her head back down over the curtains and tried to concentrate harder.

The next day, Ellie was determined to find out whatever might be troubling Caleb. To her delight, when she arrived at the log cabin site, he was already on the porch waiting for her. His brothers were busy doing all sorts of things in the background and she could hear the sounds of a saw, hammers, and the usual cheerful banter among them. When Caleb saw her, he jumped down from the porch over the side of the rail and put his finger to his lips, indicating she should be quiet. She smiled and nodded, her green eyes sparkling to see he was back to his normal self. He took her free hand in his and quickly drew her away from the cabin toward the woods before his brothers could spot them.

When he realized she could barely keep up with his long legs, he slowed down when they were a good distance from the cabin. "A little further." He pulled her along gently, his voice still low as they progressed deeper among the peeling white birch and thick pine trees. "I've got something to show you."

Breathless, a giggle escaped from her mouth, but she nodded joyfully, realizing she completely trusted her handsome fiancé with her whole heart. "Here," she said, offering him the lunch pail which had grown too heavy. She could hardly wait to see what he had to show her. All of her previous apprehensions began to melt away and she silently chided herself for having any notions of distrust whatsoever.

Caleb stopped in a thick part of the woods and bent down to put his hands on his thighs and catch his breath. She gulped in more air and when they were both rested, he appeared to be looking for a spot where they could sit down. He spied a large log on the ground a few yards away and taking her by the hand again, led her to it and sat down, patting the spot beside him. She sat down, glad she'd worn her hair pinned up into a loose knot and tucked into her bonnet. She smoothed out the folds of her long navy skirt and pulled her pale pink shawl closer. She looked up into his blue eyes — peaceful blue — the color of a clear summer sky, eager to hear what he had to tell her.

"I've missed you," she began with a sweet smile.

"I've missed you, too. More than you know. Have you noticed anything odd these past few days?"

"You've been a little grumpy?" She giggled then at her remark.

Even he couldn't help but grin with her. "Well, yes, and I'm sorry about that, but it's been a very complex few days."

"I understand. Some days are a challenge." She tucked her arm in his. "All is forgiven, my love."

He leaned forward and kissed her on the forehead. Then he grew serious again. "Have you noticed anything else?"

"Hmm." Ellie pondered his question and then her face brightened. "Charlie! Where's Charlie been hiding lately? He's always at the cabin with you."

Caleb smiled broadly and nodded. "I knew you'd figure it out. He's been missing for days and it's really been bothering me."

"Wow, I had no idea, Caleb! Why didn't you tell me? I thought he was at home with your Ma keeping warm by the fireplace. I've been so preoccupied with our wedding plans, I didn't even realize he wasn't at the log cabin site with you like usual. He's normally such a faithful dog."

"He is, and I thought he was with Ma too, but every night I'd return home after the milking chores and he wasn't anywhere to be found. Pa, well, he's been a little demanding lately. There's all the morning milking chores to be done. Then the evening chores, too. That has been a part of my mood. We had a huge order for cheese and butter to be filled for a restaurant in town on top of the regular dairy wagon route, so he needed my brothers and I needed them, too. Then, I've been out late at night searching for Charlie on top of everything else."

"That's awful. No wonder you've been upset. It's getting really busy around our house, too." She propped her chin in her palm. "Did you find Charlie?"

He nodded. "You'll never guess where."

"Where?"

"We can't tell a soul, not yet anyhow."

"All right," she nodded, one brow furrowing in wonder.

"Charlie made a new friend out here in the woods. Pa would be really mad, and I can't tell him yet. Not 'til after the wedding. He's got a lot on his mind. You know how he feels 'bout poachers." He looked at her with that you know what I'm talking about look on his face and she nodded briskly. Pa Andrews could be a stickler about trespassers, poachers, chicken thieves, and the like.

"Do I ever!" she agreed. "So tell me about Charlie's friend."

"He's Swedish and his name's Christopher Farman. His father is Olaf Farman. He used to live on the other side of Polk County. He threw Christopher out of the house for becoming a Christian. From what I understand, Olaf doesn't believe anymore because his wife died of the influenza on the ship coming over from Sweden. He became an alcoholic and beat on Christopher. Then he eventually threw him out when he became a believer and accepted Christ."

"How old is Christopher?"

"Ten."

"That's awful! His father threw a ten-year-old boy out of the house and into the cold? It's still very chilly at night." Elizabeth's mouth dropped open as she considered the situation. "How will he survive?"

Caleb drew in a deep breath and sighed, shrugging. "I don't know. I finally ran into his campsite here in the woods looking for Charlie. He's camping up yonder about another five minutes from here. Charlie's become a loyal friend to him and I don't mind sharing, but I wanted you to know."

"He must be so cold and hungry. Have you tried to find his father?"

"Yes. Olaf has completely vanished. He doesn't live in Polk County anymore as far as we know, and he scared the boy from the idea of returning home by threatening to kill him if he ever decided to go back. From what I gather, this has been going on for about three months. Christopher—he goes by Chris sometimes—survived the rest of the winter in a cave not far from here, but he believes an angel brought him food and helped him. He's actually on his second or third camping site here in our woods."

"Wow! The Bible talks about angels the Lord sends to help us in times of danger, although I've never seen one."

"I admit, part of me has been a little hungry, too. I've been making up excuses to not eat with you so I could give him my delicious lunches you've made for me. I didn't mean to lie to you. I don't want our marriage to start out with this between us, but I had to sort it out in my head first. I'm so sorry, Ellie. Can you ever forgive me?"

Ellie threw her arms around Caleb's neck and leaned her head against his strong chest. "Oh Caleb, we have so much to share! Of course, there's no question about my forgiveness. I'm far more worried about the little boy living out here in the cold all alone in the woods. We've got to help him. We've got to take him in, as soon as we're married. Sooner if possible. I've got to speak to my parents."

"Oh, Elizabeth Jean Calhoun, I love you so much! I was just going to ask you if we could. I don't know what the law is in this situation, but he's just a child. I was hoping you'd feel the same way and I knew you'd want to help."

Tears rolled down her cheeks and Caleb put his arms on her shoulders. "I didn't mean to make you cry." He wiped away the tears tenderly and kissed her again on her forehead, drawing her back into his arms.

"It's not you, it's the whole situation," she sniffled, trying to wipe more tears away.

When she'd calmed and sat up straighter on the log, he reached for the lunch pail. "Ellie, he needs this food more than we do."

She nodded, her eyes wide, wondering what she'd find when she met Christopher. "And you've tried to find his father?"

"Only once. I couldn't get away for very long with all that's going on, but I drove the buckboard and Chris led me to the tenement where they used to live. It's completely empty. Nobody else has rented the place yet, and I believe the boy. I can't understand why his father would pour out so much hate."

"Maybe he looks like his mother and it hurts Olaf to be reminded of his loss at a time when it should give him comfort. His heart must be hard as stone since he rejects Christ and spews threats at a child who needs his love. It's so very sad. We must help him, Caleb, we must," Ellie insisted.

"Are you ready to meet him?"

She nodded again. "Yes, I'm ready."

"Are you sure? He's very thin and small for his age."

She drew in a breath of courage to face the situation. If a ten-year-old boy could face this, she could. "I'm ready."

"All right then. Let's hurry, we don't have much time. We've got to get back to the site soon. My brothers will be wondering where we are." Caleb stood up and took her by the hand, helping her rise.

"I'll bring extra lunch tomorrow," she said as he pulled her along to meet Christopher.

"You look beautiful," Louisa Edwina Calhoun said as she helped her daughter position and secure her wedding veil.

"Mama, will you tie the locket on for me?" Ellie held the ends of the blue ribbon up so her mother could tie it securely around her neck. "It's my something blue from Grandma. Thank you for making my dress. I love it! It's absolutely perfect."

"You're welcome, my darling. I can hardly believe it's your wedding day. Seems like yesterday when I held you in my arms for the first time." Mama wiped a tear from her eyes and they stood back to admire her gown together.

Grandma entered the room and paused, her hand covering her mouth. "Oh, you're a vision of heaven. I love your hair up like that and the wreath of violets, white roses, and sweet pea in your hair. You're a lovely bride, Elizabeth. Your veil, the dress, the locket—you look stunning."

"Thank you Grandma, and thank you for my locket." Ellie looked nervously around the bedroom, realizing she'd spent her last night in the pleasant bedroom as a maiden. If she visited her childhood home in the future, it would be as Mrs. Caleb Andrews. "Has Mary Jo finished readying our ring bearer?"

"Yes, that's what I came to tell you." Grandma smiled and poked her head out into the narrow hall leading to the other three bedrooms. "Come in, Christopher."

Christopher gingerly stepped into the room, bathed, fed, and dressed in a white shirt and a little black suit to match Caleb's. "How do I look?"

"Christopher," Ellie breathed a smile, "you look so handsome. Ready to be our ring bearer?"

"Ja," he nodded, a huge grin on his shiny, clean face. "Thanks for taking me in, Miss Ellie."

"You're most welcome," she replied. "Did you know Christopher means bearer of Christ and the name of Farman has origins which mean traveling merchant? I looked it up in a book of names at the library."

His eyes grew wide. "Ja, I do ever since the angel told me, but I'd forgotten—until now."

Ellie smiled. "And do you think you can be happy with Caleb and me?"

He nodded vigorously. "Ja, I do."

She knelt down to look him in the eyes. "Now Christopher, Caleb and I will be going away on our honeymoon to a romantic place in Canada. When we return, in about a fortnight, that's fourteen days, we'll pick you up and take you home with us to live in our new cabin. My family will look after you until then, and you may sleep in my room, all right? Can you be very brave until we return?"

He nodded and gave her a wide grin revealing one missing front tooth. Other than the missing tooth, he looked exactly how she imagined Caleb might have looked at his age with golden hair and blue eyes.

She stood up straight, smoothed her dress, accepted her bouquet of white roses from her mother standing patiently by, and held out her arm. "All right then. If you don't mind, would you kindly escort me to the carriage?"

"Sure, ja, I will," he smiled, clasping his arm around hers.

Balloons at Sunrise

Krystine Kercher

In the still air of pre-dawn, the flight crew for the Desert Belle unfolded and spread the nylon envelope over the dew-heavy grass. Street lamps at the edge of the field gave a faint illumination, aided by the steady glare of truck headlights, and flashlights and headlamps bobbing all over the field as flight crews for other balloons prepared their craft for takeoff.

Desert Belle's crew consisted of Cooper Pawson, his wife Gina, and their friends, Tomas and Anita Fuentes.

While Tomas and Anita inspected the envelope, Cooper grabbed a set of steel load cables and secured them to one side of the basket waiting nearby while Gina secured the others. The anchor rope was already in place, tied to a metal stake driven deep into the ground.

He hopped up into the back of the truck and lifted a twenty pound propane cylinder down into her waiting hands. "Who are you taking up this morning?"

"A family of four—the Stevens. Lily and Dave, and their kids Hunter and Penny."

Cooper whistled through his teeth as he grabbed two more propane cylinders and passed them down too.

The best part of owning a hot air balloon is flying in it. The worst part of owning one is the expense. The crew's solution was to take turns flying the balloon while giving paying guests a ride. Desert Belle could easily lift six people. If two of them were experienced balloonists, that left room for four guests.

With the need to cover insurance as well as the repair costs and fuel, the Pawsons and the Fuentes doubled their fees when children came aboard. At balloon fests like this one, interested spectators could arrange to ride for a fee. The Stevens had to be pretty motivated to cover the resulting fare.

Tomas climbed into the basket as Cooper jumped down from the truck, and helped Gina over the edge. Cooper took his place in walking the envelope and adjusting the folds as Tomas and Gina began to fill the envelope with hot air from the burners. They roared in the pre-dawn stillness.

Anita came around the bulge of the balloon and gave Cooper two thumbs up. "Looking good," she said as she wiped dirt from her hands with a rag that she tucked in the hip pocket of her coveralls.

"Are you ready to fly today?"

Anita grinned. "Are you sorry you aren't going up?" She and Gina would be flying the balloon while Tomas and Cooper tracked their progress with the truck.

Cooper flashed a regretful smile her way. "There's always next time. You watch out for those kids."

"Hopefully they'll listen and be good for us." Anita grabbed another fold and shook it out as Cooper walked down the envelope and tugged a vertical load tape.

"Riding with us is a privilege, not a right. If they don't listen on the ground, Tomas will go with you."

"But Gina—"

"There will always be another time."

Anita nodded.

The balloon inflated in a lopsided fashion—inevitable given its previously flattened state. Cooper followed Anita around the balloon to the other side, where they pulled and tugged some more until the envelope pulled free of the ground.

The faintest bit of color tinted the sky in the east, waking a wide array of colors from the balloons bobbing all across the field. Desert Belle's envelope rose overhead, displaying alternating panels of dusty purple, rose, and gold.

"Here come our passengers," Gina called, perched on the edge of the basket. She unrolled the short rope ladder that customers used to climb into the basket.

Tomas bailed out on the other side and came around to join Cooper and Anita as the foursome arrived with an event guide and ten other people.

The guide initialed his checklist, and looked around. "Who's the captain for this flight?"

Anita stepped forward. "I am." She signed the form, then shook hands with the Stevens.

Lily gripped a hand from each of her children. The kids still looked a little sleepy, although the boy—Hunter—was bouncing up and down on his toes.

"Listen up! These are the rules you must abide by if you wish to fly in our balloon…" Anita went through the rules, then had the Stevens sign some legal paperwork. She gave the paperwork to Cooper who tucked it into the flight folder.

Cooper and Tomas steadied the ladder so that the kids and their parents could climb aboard. Anita climbed up last, then rolled up the ladder. Tomas untied the anchor rope while Cooper climbed into the cab of the truck, stowed the folder, and started the truck.

The sun broke over the horizon. As the Desert Belle lifted off and drifted away from the field, Tomas rode shotgun as they drove across the field, joining a line of other vehicles that followed their balloonists.

In the balloon, the kids oohed and ahhed at the sights as the gondola floated low over the city sleeping below them. The noisy burners brought people out of their homes in their pj's and robes to smile and wave, and take photos. Dave Stevens waved back and took photos of the people looking up. He also took photos of his wife Lily, who had turned an unfortunate shade of green but tried to smile anyway, and of his kids.

"Can you take a photo of us?" He shoved the camera into Gina's hands.

"We're too low. We need to go higher to avoid the power lines coming up," Anita said.

Gina set the burners to a full-throated roar before she snapped several shots and handed the camera back.

"Mr. Stevens, please keep Hunter in the basket. We wouldn't want him falling overboard," Anita warned as Hunter leaned over the edge.

Dave ignored her in favor of snapping more photos, but Lily grabbed for Hunter and pulled him down into the basket.

"Awww—Mo-om!"

"You listen to me, Hunter Stevens! If you ever want to ride in a hot air balloon again, you do what the captain says," Lily hissed at him.

Penny smirked and stuck out her tongue at Hunter.

"Why, you—" Hunter threw himself at Penny, rocking the basket.

Lily yanked him back and moaned, "I think I'm going to be sick…"

Dave put down the camera and frowned at his son. "Hunter James Stevens."

"Yes, Dad." Hunter hung his head.

"That goes for you too, young lady."

Penny's smirk disappeared. She patted her mom's arm and turned back to peering over the top of the basket.

Lily sagged against the side of the basket, eyes closed, a hand to her mouth as she breathed deeply.

Gina fumbled in the breast pocket of her flight suit and snagged a foil-coated plastic pack. She offered it to Lily. "Mrs. Stevens, would you like some Dramamine?"

Their course followed an air current they had ridden before. It held true, and a few minutes later they landed on a nice rise a few miles outside of town, where Cooper and Tomas joined them in the truck. While the men and Gina deflated the balloon, Anita gave the Stevens a ride back to their SUV.

Cooper watched his wife smiling as she flattened and folded the balloon's envelope into a neat package and decided that the trip had been a success. There would be more flights. Next time, he'd be the one flying the balloon. He couldn't wait.

Susan's Angry Again

Jude Kandace Laughe

No matter how often anyone did something for Susan, she could be angry again a heartbeat later. She just wasn't happy unless she was stirring up trouble.

Her mother often referred to her as a drama queen, or a pink princess. Susan didn't like it. But she did nothing to solve the problem.

After a while of being angry, Susan often disappeared into her shell to worry out her anger, and fuss. The problem of Susan's anger had been felt by most in her life, but nobody knew how to solve the problem.

Susan occasionally said she wanted to be less angry, but she rarely acted on her desire.

At least, until now…

Susan stood on the dock, staring out into the fog that hung over Lake Montague. The water was dark, foreboding, and still as glass. If there'd been anything to reflect, it might have been a mirror.

There was nothing. The fog hid the skies from view, and replaced the mountains surrounding the lake with dark empty space. Susan stared across the dark surface as if she could see something in the deep beyond.

Hands in her pockets, she gripped them into tight fists. She wanted to pound something, but there was nothing to pound.

She seethed in anger.

What was she angry about?

That question hounded her day and night. She had no answer. No response. She had no reason to be angry. But she felt anger powering up inside, building, growing, as if it controlled her.

Overpowered by the feeling, she spun on her heels and walked back to the shore, stepped off the dock and walked along the gravel path that led back to the cabin. She'd arrived at the family cabin two days earlier and managed to start a fire in the fireplace to warm her that first night. But now... the wood supply would dwindle out before she used much more, and she longed for a less strenuous method of finding heat.

The furnace came on almost instantly when she turned up the thermostat. The dusty warm aroma of heat filled the room, and Susan settled into the lounge by the front window. Watching the fog was a pleasant way to spend her day, but she felt angry that there wasn't sunshine. She kicked away the blanket and pushed herself out of the lounge, then stood staring at the window.

She focused on the glass, three layers of glass between her and the wooden deck. She focused in on each layer, wondering what was between the glasses.

In a moment, the rage inside her rose up and escaped, building to a red glow between the first two layers of glass. She watched as the flaming red heat of her anger grew arms, legs, and a generic face with dark eyes, a unibrow, and a cursed flat pair of lips that might have spoken had the anger been outside the glass. She spun away from the red heat of anger and walked across the room.

Stopping near the stair railing, she looked back to see the anger glowing hot, building between the glass, and taking form.

"I command you to be gone!" She spoke in a loud demanding voice, rushing up the stairs away from the heat.

On the second floor, Susan stopped and glanced back. She watched as the anger melted between the glasses and slid to the bottom to hover at the lower edge of the window. Still red hot, anger contained by the glass.

Susan flopped across the bed and laid there with her eyes closed. She held her breath momentarily, then raised her face, and sucked in the cool air from the second floor. She stared at the lazy wedding ring pattern on the quilt and wondered if her grandmother had used fabric from any of her dresses in the tiny squares. She didn't recognize any of the patterns, but her grandmother often salvaged fabric from clothing to make her quilts. Susan pulled at a loose thread and snapped it off, removing a few stitches in the process. She didn't care. Nobody would notice.

She wandered through the rooms on the second floor, stopping occasionally to look at framed photos. Some included her on the banks of Lake Montague, others were of her brother, Glenn, or Samantha. She stared at a photo of the three of them sitting on the dock, legs hanging almost to the water, Glenn with an arm around each of them. He looked happy.

Samantha was smiling, almost laughing.

Susan looked angry, as if she wanted him to let her go.

The photos had been in color once upon a time, now they were faded, almost to white. She stared at them, wondering why they faded so fast. The bigger question was her anger. Why was she so angry?

"Wasn't I ever happy?" She asked the vacant space on the third floor, as if someone there might answer her. "Why could everyone else be happy, but I was always so angry?"

You were never content…

Her mother's words rose up from the dust on the third level wood floors. Susan sat down on a wooden bench by the only window on the third floor and stared out across the foggy lake. Nothing was really visible, just a haze of fog wrapping around the cabin.

"Samantha had everything!" Susan shouted, screaming into the fog. "She was pretty, smart, and she had everyone's attention. Nobody wanted to spend time with me!"

Susan let angry hot tears roll unhindered down her cheek, dripping off her chin. She'd struggled with those thoughts for so long, and now she was letting them out. She wanted to let them go. A hiccupping sigh escaped, and she repeated, "Nobody wanted me."

Susan twirled the blonde ringlets that hung past her shoulder with one hand, aimlessly pulling tiny strands. Her fingers tightened on a strand and she pulled it hard, feeling the pain of her hair being pulled, but refusing to react. She pulled harder.

"Why didn't anyone want me?" She screamed into the void.

Susan flipped open the lid of a wooden trunk, bound with leather bindings, and creaky old hinges. She pushed the lid back against the railing and started looking through the contents. A baby book with Samantha's name on the cover was the first thing she pulled out. Flipping through the pages, she found intricately written memories of Samantha's first steps, of her first words, and pictures of the first months after she was born. Her mother's tight, small, even script filled nearly every page.

A white christening gown carefully wrapped in tissue paper, and then in plastic came out next. Susan unfolded the layers, dropping an envelope on the floor from the middle folds. She reached down and picked it up, then opened it. Inside she found three certificates, acknowledging the Christening events of all three, Samantha, Glenn, and Susan. A small folded note had been placed between the documents.

Susan read the words,

My darling babies, my deepest desire from the earliest memories was to have children, and have them Christened in my Christening gown. This precious white dress has been kept for this occasion, and eventually, for you to use when christening your own children. It was fashioned by your Grandmother Joyce for my sister Connie. Connie never had any children, so I was blessed to wear it myself, and then receive it to allow you each to wear on your special day. On the day I dedicated my precious darling children to the Lord, for His service. I pray you each find blessing in this moment, and in this memory. Much love, Mama

She hugged the dress to her chest, smelling the musty rose scent of it. A lingering of the rose soap her mother often used for delicate items. Susan reveled in the aroma.

Another book, with Glenn's name on the cover. Inside perfect script, page after page of memories written, recorded for the future. She thumbed through the pages, appreciating each written word. Glenn was the kind of brother every little girl wanted. Except he picked on Susan relentlessly. She always thought he preferred Samantha over her. They were closer in age, only eighteen months apart, and then Susan had been an afterthought... Almost four years later, she'd arrived on the scene and Glenn often referred to her as his "problem sister" introducing her to his friends as ornery little Susan.

She'd hated being called ornery.

Thinking back, she remembered putting sand in his bed, and filling his shoes up with his Lego pieces. She probably deserved the name. But she wasn't sure if the name came before she started pulling tricks on him, or after. Just remembered when he had introduced her to his best friend Jim from college, anger rose up in her throat like vomit. She'd been smitten from the moment she saw Jim get out of his car, and then the introduction.

"And this is my ornery little sister, Susan that I warned you about!" Glenn had mussed her hair with one hand as he gave her a one armed hug, in greeting.

Susan had felt the embarrassed look Jim gave her. He already hated her, just because Glenn labeled her ornery. She was seething, and didn't bother to give him more than a grunt in greeting before she took off running down the street.

Running.

The one thing she'd always been good at, and it saved her from so many embarrassing situations. Those running shoes. Her mother had hated that she wore them with everything. And always took off running at the most inopportune moments. Her mother had accused her more than once of running away from life.

Jim had barely spoken to her the rest of his visit in their home. Susan kept her distance. She hadn't wanted to embarrass him any more with her presence. Glenn had made a scene one afternoon, accusing her of being rude to him. So she became even more scarce. She couldn't imagine her presence was wanted after that!

Anger welled up in her again, and she longed to find an outlet.

As she exited the room, her fisted hand pummeled the wall. Solid pine held its own, and she felt the jolt all the way to her elbow. She cringed at the pain, but relished the feeling of letting off some steam.

Downstairs she sought a way to express herself with less pain.

Old stacks of magazines needed shredding, so she obliged, careful to avoid any glances at the angry red glass. After shredding the magazines, she bundled them with string and stuck them in the fire place to burn. Some she saved back to use as fire starter later, but the bulk of the mess, she set on fire and watched the colorful flames created by the ink and shellac on the paper.

Hunger pangs sent her to the kitchen, where she found a can of soup to warm on the stove. The slamming of doors, slamming of the pan onto the burner, and ultimately the splashing of the soup into a bowl had eased some of her anger too. Everything she did appeared to be an expression of her frustration with the deck life had dealt her, until she settled at the table and burned her lip on the first bite.

Tears again. Washing down her face with frustration as she pushed back from the table.

Her determined spin away from the table sent her face to face with the red hot anger in the window. A dark and brooding face looked back at her, demanding her attention. She stood there staring at the window. She couldn't see beyond the anger held tight between the glasses.

Had she looked beyond, she might have seen the fog rising. A first glimpse of mountains on the other side of the lake, or maybe noted the snow on the peaks? But she didn't bother to look past the anger.

She stopped and stared at the anger, allowing the heat of her own emotions to rise up again. Flushed with the heat of it all, Susan felt incapable of anything less than a full on assault of anguish.

White hot hatred filled her up, overflowing from her in the wake of all the anguish she'd faced during the day she'd spent reveling in her own angry thoughts. She'd been too focused on all the wrongs, to notice any of the good that had happened in her life.

Now bawling into the pillow on the couch, she'd curled into a fetal ball, weeping wildly, screaming out as if tormented by a pain of her own making. Susan succumbed to the discontent that held her hostage, and slept until deep into the dark night.

In the darkness, winds howled. The fog of the previous day was replaced by snow laden clouds, and flurries of white flakes covering the windows in frost.

Red hot anger cooled. Frost covered the outside of the window, and snow drifts hid the cabin from the roadway to the east.

Susan awakened to the first winter blizzard, and a power outage that would leave the cabin dark for days. She found candles, and brought in the last of the wood from the shed, hoping it would get her through until there was something more than wood for heat.

She let out a sigh of relief that there was still gas for the cook stove. She'd be able to prepare simple meals, at least.

A spark of gratitude helped her feel a bit better. But it was only a spark, and just for the gas that would light the stove.

Before long, Susan was bemoaning her choice to come to the cabin.

By the end of the fourth day of solitude, Susan found herself wishing for someone to come rescue her. But she'd told nobody she was coming here. She didn't think they'd care enough to come anyway.

She found books to read, and sorted through more of the things her mother had stored in the trunk upstairs, finding nothing with any real value to her. She left the things strewn about in the attic, and didn't bother to put them away again. They were things that didn't matter to her.

Her anger quickly turned to self-loathing pity as she struggled with her own emotions. The warmth of the wood fire had lasted, but she was using it sparingly, often resorting to burning the junk paper left from her mother's years of magazine collecting. Nobody wanted those anyway.

On the fifth day, as she shredded more magazines, she dropped one to the floor. Opened to an article near the middle of the page, Susan recognized a familiar photo on a page corner. She stopped shredding and began to read the article beside the photo.

Three or four paragraphs below the start of the article, she read,

"Susan loves our long haired mutt, but her short little fingers get caught in his fur and he snaps at her. We've had to keep a close eye on him, and keep her away from him when nobody is near, to prevent him from nipping her tender skin. She gets so upset when we don't let her play with him. But she doesn't understand that his skin is sensitive due to his medication, and she's still toddler-rough when she plays. She's such an adorable little tyke, and he just adores her. It's hard to keep them apart."

Susan scanned through the article, remembering the dog in the picture. She had thought the dog didn't like her, because he always snapped at her, nipping at her arms. She'd stopped liking dogs after that, since they didn't like her. She just couldn't bring herself to pet them, or love them.

Several paragraphs down, Susan read,

"Samantha brought her best friend home from school today. Susan hung out with them, until they were getting ready to go out. At thirteen, their first dates were as a group with friends, and Susan wanted to go with them so bad. I think they might have taken her if they'd had an extra ticket. They all thought she was adorable in that gray ruffled hoodie, and sweat pants. Even after one of the kids called to try to get another ticket, and they were sold out, Josie offered to skip the event so Susan could go. But that just wouldn't have been fair. After all, Susan would have her chance to go on a group date when she got a little older. I love how all of Samantha's friends just adore Susan. We may not have planned to have our little Suzie Cherub, but we are so blessed to have her in our lives."

Susan let the tears run down her cheeks.

She hadn't realized the kids wanted her to go as much as she'd wanted to go with them. Or that the reason she hadn't been allowed to go was that they couldn't get another ticket.

The anger she'd felt earlier had diminished greatly by the time she found Glenn's treasure box in the dresser in his room, on the seventh day of her seclusion.

There were shells, coins, a pocket knife, and photos, but in the bottom of the box was an envelope full of folded notes. Susan sorted through the notes, looking over her shoulder as if Glenn might walk in on her at any moment. She'd sorted through several thank you notes, and short messages from friends, before she found one from Jim.

"Glenn, Thanks for the invite to spend the weekend with your family. I had really looked forward to meeting Susan, from all the fun things we'd talked about, I thought she might be someone I'd really like. And I did. She was adorable, but evidently she didn't like me to run off so fast. I guess she wasn't impressed by how shy I am… I was hoping, though. Thanks again for the invite. I'd love to visit your home again sometime, maybe I can make a better impression. Jim"

Susan stared at the letter. Jim thought she hadn't liked him because he was shy… She thought back over the introduction, and remembered how embarrassed Jim had looked when Glenn introduced them. She thought he'd been embarrassed because Glenn was introducing him to HER. She hadn't realized Jim was shy at all. She just thought he didn't like her.

Tears ran down her cheeks, and she sat there silent on the side of the bed.

A week in this house, and other than her own anger and hatred for herself, she hadn't found one bit of evidence that her family hated her. The realization brought more tears. She swiped them away wishing she could escape the pain of her own anger, and take back some of those thoughts… Maybe she could take back some of the anger?

Carefully, she replaced Glenn's things in his treasure box and placed it back in the top drawer of the dresser. She longed to talk to her brother, but she still couldn't get her car past the snow drift that covered the entrance to the driveway. She spent the afternoon sipping coffee and thinking about digging her way out. She wondered if there was a shovel in the shed, or if she'd be able to get to it.

When morning came the next day, she was dressing warmly in her coat and scarf, wearing a pair of Glenn's warm hiking boots, and searching through the shed for a shovel. She found one hanging on the side wall, waiting for her to use it. She'd dug her way through one snow drift and found the snow plows had blown past, leaving another small drift to dig through. She'd worked her way through that one before midafternoon, and went back to check the cabin.

All was in order, she closed it all up, shut off the lights, and carried her bags to the Jeep she'd driven up the mountain over a week earlier.

Susan drove down the mountain, arriving back in the city well after dark. Her brother lived several miles east of her on the other side of the city, but she was determined to get there before bedtime.

Glenn was sitting in the living room when she pulled into his drive, reading the evening paper with his feet up on the coffee table. She watched through the window for a moment, admiring the way he studied the paper, and still glanced back at his wife practicing on the piano. He and Karen had been married nearly a year and Susan hadn't known she played the piano. She'd never visited their home.

She rolled her eyes when she remembered that she'd barely made it to their wedding, and she hadn't stayed for much of the reception, afraid she'd run into Glenn's best man, Jim.

She pushed open the door of her jeep and walked up to the door.

Glenn opened the door moments later, and welcomed her inside.

"Hey, squirt! What are you doing here?" He asked.

Susan recognized his question as having genuine interest in why she was standing there. "I just thought it was time I came to check out your new house!"

Karen had joined him at the door the minute she heard Susan's name. "Come in, Susan! It's so good to see you!"

"Good to see both of you too." Susan answered, "I had gone to the cabin before it started snowing, and when I drove back down the mountain, I just wanted to see you."

"I'm glad you're here." Glenn welcomed her into his home, "Have you had dinner? We had the best stew. Karen is an amazing cook."

"Oh, let me get you a bowl, it will warm you up." Karen was already off to the kitchen before Susan could answer.

"Any left for me?" Another voice made Susan look toward the stairwell into the basement, "I just finished, and was coming up to see if there was any dinner left?" Jim stood at the top of the stairs.

"Susan, you remember my friend, Jim? He's staying here while he gets settled into his new job." Glenn introduced them again, this time without referring to her as ornery, or little.

"I do. So good to see you again, Jim!" Susan stretched out her hand. "No runners, I can't take off on an Olympic Sprint this time!" She pointed to Glenn's hiking boots still on her feet.

"Good, perhaps I can get to know you this time?" Jim added.

South Dakota Foreman

E. V. Sparrow

Worried dark Macedonian eyes held the terrified blue gaze of the pale Irishman. Ace shook his head. "I know not…tell you Borko's plan." He shuffled his feet. "You go, run fast."

"Ta where? There's no place ta go. They'll find me on the open plains or kill ya for tellin' me their plan."

Ace sat on the box spring mattress. "They come at night. You go? Yes?"

"Yes, yes. I don't want ta die! You gave me time ta escape by tellin' me." Maurice paced back and forth, his winter boots scuffed the floor. "But how?"

"I say no, Borko, boss not steal your money. He good boss."

"I would show them the telegram, but they cannot read English." Maurice snatched it off his desk, "The railroad clearly states that a blizzard snowed in the tracks further east, delaying our paychecks by one day." Maurice regarded Ace. "The men know the winter in South Dakota is harsh...they've been working here for a while." The telegram trembled in Maurice's hand.

Ace stared at it.

"What if ya tell them their pay'll be here in the mornin'? Maurice shook the paper at Ace. "Do ya think they'd wait?"

"No. They not wait."

Maurice sat on his wooden chair in his cold one-room boxcar and held his head in his hands. Rivulets of sweat trickled from under his bright red hair and between his fingers. "The railroad's Yard Force just promoted me as Foreman. Now this." What do I do? I can't protect myself from twenty-four grown men. He lowered his hands and raised his gaze to his only friend, Ace. "What shall I do?"

They mad. They say you thief. They not care." Ace clenched his fists and frowned. "They hang boss at night. You run! Go to town?"

"Town? Tis only a supply town, Ace. Three buildings and four men." Maurice flopped onto his mattress. "Do ya think 'tis possible a U. S. Marshall could be there? Ace, me best hope is if ya return ta the crew and play the innocent. I'll devise a plan. Hold them off as long as ya can. Go, Ace."

"I go, boss." Ace hesitated and studied Maurice until he shut the boxcar door.

Maurice rose and clasped his hands on the top of his head. "Tis impossible! Dear God in heaven, help me." Think. He took a few deep breaths. Think. "If Ya rescue me from this evil plot, I'll serve Ya all of me days of me life, I swear!" Maurice paced the edge of his room. His gaze landed on the bottles of whisky he'd purchased for Pa's Christmas gift. Maurice froze. "Glory be, tis the answer!"

Maurice's older sister, Mary, stood at the small glass window in their homestead's kitchen. She stared at her reflection against the whiteness beyond and listened to the wind that howled like a banshee. "This wind tis so awful, tis blowin' snow off the ground and makin' it bare in places."

Margaret's reflection joined hers in the window, and then Josephine's appeared, chest high in front of them.

Mary flipped her long, bright red braid off her shoulder. It smacked against Margaret's chin and whacked Jo's forehead. Mary giggled, "Tis the most fun I've had in days."

The sisters scowled, then giggled.

Loud snores interrupted the girls.

Margaret lay a finger on her lips, "Shh. Don't wake Pa. He's been so grumpy lately."

The three girls regarded the empty whisky bottle sitting on the worn kitchen table. Mary sighed and whispered, "Whisky is his music ta relax him and lull him to sleep. Ever since Ma left us, Pa's love is whisky." At the younger girls' shocked expressions, Mary added, "No since denyin' what 'tis right in front of our eyes."

"Pa likes ta drink, dat he does." Margaret fidgeted with her lace collar, then turned back to watch the windblown snow. "Do ya wonder what happened ta Maurice? I feel a bit uneasy. Tis a strange thing not ta hear from him. He always brings us money on da mornin' of his payday."

Josephine twisted a lock of hair. "Do ya think somethin's happened to him, then?" She bit her lip and watched Margaret's face.

"Ah, no." Mary shook her head at Margaret over the top of Josephine's. "He's only a few hours late, darlin'."

Pa awoke. "What are ya girls a whisperin' about?"

"We were just speakin' about Maurice. He was due taday," Mary called out.

Josephine skipped to her Pa's chair and lay her hand on his shoulder. "But we are not ta worry. He's only a bit late, Pa."

"Tis true. Not ta worry. He's a good boy. Tis why the railroad just made him Foreman at eighteen." Pa smiled and closed his eyes.

Ace approached the crew's boxcar. His boots crunched on the frozen ground. Loud voices from the boxcar blew past him on the wind. He knew he'd not sleep tonight after what Borko and the crew planned to do to his boss-friend. Two men against twenty-four? Ace knew the men, he was one of them. He spoke the language, but he didn't trust them to wait for their pay. The crew didn't yet trust Maurice.

Ace turned and scanned the horizon. The sun was a few hours from dipping below it. The big snowstorm had passed through several days ago. At their end of the rails they received only a dusting of snow, but the Railroad said it snowed feet deep further east. That's why it was hard for the men to believe that the snow held up the train.

The boxcar door opened and Borko stood framed inside it. His eyes widened, then narrowed at Ace. He spread his stance, and Borko spoke in their language, "So where have you been, Ace? We could not find you. Were you with your friend, the thief?" He sneered, his jaw clenched.

More men dressed in thick work coats joined Borko. Some of their expressions were hostile, some were afraid.

Borko likes us to fear him. Ace thought of Maurice and explained, "Needed some privacy…for…you know. Since our outhouse burnt down. Had to move barrels." He attempted a grin.

Someone chuckled.

Borko tapped his hand clutching the coil of rope against his other hand. He stepped aside and announced, "You stay here with the rest of us while we await sunset." Borko slammed the door. "After we hang the boss, we will search his boxcar for our money. We know he has it hidden there. You will join us, Ace."

Ace nodded. He couldn't think of anything he could do to help Maurice. He stuffed his emotions, removed his work cap, and set it on a barrel. Mob mentality is a dangerous way to deal with troubles. Boss is right, he cannot hide, the land is flat and barren. Things were going to get ugly and deadly, and there was nothing Ace could do about it. God, help Maurice.

"The odds are against me, but if I can count Ya in God, it could work." Will whiskey stall them til mornin'? What other weapons do I have that won't harm me men? Maurice scanned his belongings inside the boxcar. Snow shovel. A chair. Some blankets. The lantern, and me savings. But not enough to pay the men. He turned his thoughts outside. Me horse. One supply wagon. Two hours of daylight. Even though his crew wished to harm him, he didn't wish to harm the men.

More whiskey. Maurice nodded and calculated the distance to the supply "town." 'Tis near enough ta reach before dark. Maybe there'll be a marshal there. If not, I need ta find a weapon in town, or they may kill Ace. Maurice's heart pounded. He spun around. Can I hitch Biller ta the wagon without raisin' an alarm? He decided to come up with a good story. No. No. T'would be best ta tell Borko we need supplies. That'll seem less suspicious.

The wind howled in waves around Maurice's boxcar.

Maurice snatched his roll of cash and stashed it in his jacket pocket. He grabbed his shovel in case the wagon wheels got stuck in the snow. "So, if You're with me, God? Let us get on with it." He shoved his work cap onto his head and lifted the fur collar of his jacket tight against his neck. Maurice crossed himself and announced, "Borko, I pray ya believe me tale."

Biller whinnied his greeting at Maurice's approach. The black horse nodded his head and danced in his stall.

The wind blew through the slats of weathered wood in the small barn, but Maurice lit the lantern easily enough.

He listened for sounds and rubbed Biller's muzzle. Maurice flattened his cash, stashed it under the heavy blanket, and cinched it on snug with a strap around Biller. Maybe Borko won't think ta check under the blanket. He gathered more blankets that had just a bit of horse smell on them and piled them in the wagon.

A coyote howled in the distance, and Biller's ears twitched forward and back. He snorted and quivered.

"All's well. Think I've come ta feed ya?" Maurice seized the tackle and hitched Biller to the wagon. "Tis a work day, Biller. Ya ready for an adventure, boyo?"

Biller shook his long black mane.

"You're a good boyo. Hold up a minute." Maurice whispered near Biller's ear. "I need ta take ya ta the enemy first. Be me guard?" Maurice led Biller and the wagon toward the men's boxcar. When they were several feet away, the door opened.

"Here we go," Maurice whispered to Biller. "Get ready. God, 'tis time 'ta help."

A grizzled Borko stepped out the door and stood with gloved hands on his hips. He jerked his head toward Maurice, and Ace followed him outside.

Borko growled something at Ace. Ace nodded and turned pale. "Boss, the men and Borko, say where you go?"

"I came ta tell ya we need supplies." Maurice noticed Ace flinch. "Does anyone wish ta go into town with me?" Maurice smiled. "I could use the company."

Ace translated for Borko.

Maurice kept Biller and the wagon between himself and the men. "We're losin' daylight fast. I got ta return by dark. Any takers?"

Borko jerked his head toward Maurice and spoke to Ace. He scowled and glanced between them as they spoke in English.

Ace frowned. "Boss, Borko say he want search you for our money." Ace shoved his hands in his jacket pockets. "You say yes, they say you go."

"Okay. Tis fine by me. Can Borko come ta me? I need ta hold Biller. The wind spooks him most times. He might start a kickin'." *God, use their fear of me horse ta keep them in check.*

Biller snorted, sidestepped, and jingled his reins.

"Good boyo," Maurice murmured.

The men bumped into each other and scrambled a few paces back.

Borko motioned to two others to join him. They all kept out of Biller's reach. The three men searched Maurice's jacket, trousers, gloves, and pulled off his boots and socks. They even shook out the blankets in the wagon.

"Tis gettin' mighty cold. Can I have me jacket and socks, now?" Maurice called out to Ace.

Borko yanked off Maurice's cap and looked inside. He grumbled something to Ace.

"Men say want to search your boxcar," Ace translated. "You say yes, they say go."

"Fine, Ace. But, tell them don't break anythin' and they can have the whiskey. It'll warm them up till I get back."

Borko's hard, black gaze impaled Maurice. He grunted, stepped back, and waved his arm toward the supply town.

Ace yelled, "Boss, you have plan?"

"Yes, Ace. I do." Maurice slapped the reins against Biller's furry back, and hollered at Ace, "If God will do His part!"

Blue sky glowed through the break in the clouds that scuttled above the plains.

"Biller, there never was a better horse than you. Me apologies for makin' ya out ta be a bad one." Maurice slapped the reins on Biller's neck again. "Let's fly!"

In 1916, their nearest town on the plains consisted of a stable, a saloon, and a supply store. Each building had one owner — three men, besides Maurice.

At the stable, Maurice loosened the strap which held the saddle blanket, removed his cash from under it, and handed Biller off to the stable boy. "He needs a good walk, a brush, and then a drink. I'll be in the saloon and return in half an hour."

The sun was still above the plains, but it was going down in a glorious blaze of orange, purple, and gold-rimmed clouds. Faint piano notes, and off-key singing, drifted from the saloon's open door.

"Time to enact me plan." Maurice entered the empty saloon looking for Stan, but two women sashayed up to him.

"Well, if it isn't Maurice. Where have you been?" asked a brunette woman with large doe eyes.

He removed his cap. "Hello, Amy. Workin' as usual." Maurice's fair skin flushed from his neck up. "Where's Stan? Can ya get him for me?"

Amy sauntered to a door at the back of the saloon and glanced back at Maurice.

"Ah, the railway is his mistress, still." The golden-blonde winked.

"Yeah Sally, as always." Maurice didn't recognize one younger woman in a velvety pink dress.

The woman in pink smiled and touched her piled up brown hair.

He glanced quickly away. Ya know why I'm here, God. To get the marshal.

"Hey, Maurice! It's been a few months, yeah?" Stan emerged from the doorway and shook Maurice's hand. "What brings you to town? The store closed early."

"Can we speak alone?" Maurice stepped toward the bar.

"Looks like you got troubles. Is that right, Maurice?" Stan waved the girls to a round table near the wall.

"Yeah, troubles. Lookin' for a marshal. Is he here?"

Stan leaned against the counter. "No, he's not due back until later this month. He's about fifty-miles away."

Maurice calculated—three men in town, plus some women. "Got any customers here, upstairs I mean?" Maurice flushed.

"No. Been quiet this past week. Why are you curious about my customers?"

Maurice shrugged. So, four men in town, plus me and Ace. Very outnumbered.

Stan regarded Maurice. "Heard there was a blizzard. Kept most men away without the train able to get through. But you'd know that better than anyone." He grabbed a bottle and held it up.

"No, thanks." Maurice fidgeted with his coat sleeve. "Well, part of me problem is the snow on the rails." Maurice ran his fingers through his hair.

Stan poured himself a glass and wiped the counter. "You never drink. I always offer, and you always say no." Stan grinned.

"Me Pa drinks. I get his bottles at the store. Do ya have an extra case of whisky I can purchase from ya?"

Stan choked on his drink and spewed it onto the bar. He wiped his mouth on his sleeve. "A case? Think so."

Giggles erupted from the table, catching Maurice's attention.

Weapons—whisky and…women? "How many girls do ya have a workin' here now, Stan?" Maurice asked.

Stan's jaw dropped. "What? First you ask…what are you…you showed no interest in my ladies of the evening before." Stan's expression revealed his struggle to contain his laughter. He pointed, "There's six—Amy and Sally. Then Rose, Frieda, Bess, and Dolly."

The ladies of the evening rose at the sound of their names and glided toward the men who studied them. Their winter dresses rustled with the swish of their steps.

"I'm wantin' to hire their services. How much would it be for all of them?"

Stan's eyes widened, and his brow disappeared into his hairline. "Hire. All?"

"Or any who are willin' to go with me."

"You must be in terrible trouble to...what's going on?" Stan leaned forward and scanned Maurice's face.

No harm must come ta anyone. "Me men are restless." It's not a lie, God. "Bad-tempered." Tis true, God. Maurice shifted his feet and considered the women. Would me men hurt these women? "Do any of ya know some of me men? Don't say a name, just give me a yes or a no."

Stan addressed the women, "You can reply if you wish."

Amy answered yes first, then Bess, Sally, Rose, and finally Frieda. Amy explained, "Dolly's new here. She hasn't seen any of them, yet."

Maurice stared at the ceiling. "Would ya say they're kind men?" He cleared his throat, "I mean, do they...are they...do they treat ya bad?"

The five women shook their heads.

"Why ask us that, Maurice?" Amy tipped her head sideways.

"I have three sisters. It matters. So, there be twenty or so men. If any of ya are willin', I need ta hire ya for the night. I'll return ya on the train tomorrow when it arrives about 7:00 am. What's your price, Stan?"

Stan murmured the price, Maurice nodded, and pulled out his cash.

Dolly, the new girl, spoke up. "I'd like to go, too." She looked to Stan.

"Leaves me with no girls, but it's quiet. Go." Stan left them to search for the case of whisky. "Meet me out front, ladies. The sun's goin' down, I'll wait for ya, but hurry." Maurice headed for Biller and the supply wagon.

The stable boy had lit the lantern and stood holding Biller in the twilight.

"Thanks, Johnny. Biller looks good." Maurice led Biller and the wagon to the saloon's door. He and Stan loaded the crate of whisky and left enough room for the women.

"A wagon ride, so fun!" Amy climbed in first. "And blankets! Such a nice thought. Our coats aren't great protection against the cold winds. We won't be cold long, will we girls?"

They giggled and made a game of innuendos.

A blessin' ta be sure, those blankets. Maurice raised his gaze to the starlit sky. "We won't make it before dark, but not ta worry ladies, the lantern will guide us." He placed it beside him on the seat. *God, take care of Ace, will Ya?*

Biller tugged the full wagon back toward the railroad's Yard Force of angry men in the boxcars.

About a quarter of a mile from the rail yard, shouts rang through the night air. Faint yellow pinpoints of light shimmered on the plain.

Maurice halted Biller at the top of a low hill, climbed down, and pulled on his lead. "Come on, boyo, let me help you go faster. There're lives at stake."

"What's all the shouting for, Maurice?" Amy leaned over the edge of the wagon.

"Ya heard me say me men are in a bad temper? Well, they are. Can ya take up the lantern for me and hold it high? And can ya girls start a callin' out? Be loud as possible. Your feminine voices will cheer them up quick." Right, God?

After the women obliged, Maurice watched the lights bob and move closer together. He couldn't hear any more shouts. Hope that's a good sign. "Biller, we're almost there. Take heart. I know you're tired. Amy, can ya hand me the lantern?"

The men stood grouped in the yard. Three held Ace in a firm grip.

Borko had his coiled rope in one hand and its looped end in the other.

Maurice halted the wagon some distance away, just in case. Where could we run anyway? He raised the lantern. "Borko, look at the supplies I brought ya."

Amy waved, "Howdy boys! Such a night to be out. Wouldn't you rather be inside?"

The horrible day was almost worth it to see the reactions on the men's faces. Rage, fear, and malice morphed into shock, hope, and joy.

Borko dropped his rope to the frozen ground. "Huh?"

The three men let go of Ace. He moved quickly away from the group and made way for them to scatter.

Forgetting their fear of Biller, several men sprinted toward the wagon when the women waved. They scuffled to be the ones to help the women down.

Maurice turned to Amy who stood beside him. "I want ya ta come get me if anyone is mean, or anythin' goes wrong. Will ya?"

Amy ran her hand along Maurice's cheek. "Kind men make up for the others. You remind me of my brother, God rest his soul. Keep treating women kindly, we need that."

Borko faced Maurice and grinned. He raised his elbow to Amy.

Amy took his arm and glanced back at Maurice. "Don't you worry, we can all take care of ourselves."

The men escorted the women to their boxcar.

Ace peered into the wagon at the case of whisky, "Help, boss? Heavy."

"Were they about ta hang ya, Ace? That's what it looked like." Maurice yanked Ace's collar down to search for marks.

Ace shook his head. "They mad. Say you no come back."

Maurice and Ace unloaded the crate. "Ace, knock on the door and tell them it's sitting out here. Someone needs ta write a song about the magic of whisky and women."

Ace smiled. "Magic."

"I need ta take care of Biller. I'll be in the stables, then off ta me car, and tryin' not ta think of the goin's on in yours. But get me if there's trouble."

"Okay, boss."

"Biller boy, ya must be tired. I'll take care of ya." Maurice led Biller and the wagon to the barn.

A train whistle blew its piercing pattern of long and then short toots.

Maurice was already up and dressed, his habit from years of working for the railway since he was a young boy. His body knew the time automatically. He stood near the barn waiting for the train's arrival.

This morning was unique due to the ladies' presence. They emerged dressed, and slightly mussed, soon after the train pulled to a stop. They squinted at the intense sunlight reflected off the shallow snow and drew their coats tight. Some of them yawned and stretched.

Ace and Borko emerged from the boxcar, and the rest of the men wandered out with the women.

Maurice approach the train slowing to a halt.

Amy led the women to the train's open door. "All is well, Maurice. Except for Dolly. I think a romance is blooming there." She tipped her head toward Dolly and the youngest man on Maurice's crew, still holding Dolly's hand. "I think they are of the same age."

"Lovesick puppy." I'll need ta keep me eye on him. Maybe Ace can help.

Amy smiled, "Thank you for offering the train. It's much too cold to ride in your wagon. You sure know how to treat a lady. May I do a favor for you in return?"

"I need to get Josephine a new coat." Maurice bit his lip. Why did I say that?

Dolly raised an eyebrow, "Josephine?"

"Me youngest sister, she's eight. She's the only one still growin' and her coat no longer fits.

It'll be her Christmas gift. If you can set one aside for me at the store, she is small for her age, then I can take care of it on me next trip into town." If I have enough saved again.

"I can do that." Amy blew a kiss and climbed the steps with the other women behind her.

The train chugged toward the west to the end of the rails, and the women waved their farewells to the crew.

Maurice took possession of the Union Railroad's cash box and turned toward his boxcar. He glanced at Borko and Ace who waited several feet away — they followed him.

Maurice sat at his table with the cash box on his right, the log book, and the sheet to sign for their pay on his left. His pen lay in the center.

The men formed their usual payday line for their money to be counted out, but they kept their gazes on the floorboards.

Maurice heard them breathing, until he called out their last names, one by one. The men's boots scuffed his floor, then they shuffled to the edge of his boxcar.

Maurice called out Borko's name. He held up the pen but clenched it tight when Borko grasped it. Borko cleared his throat, and Maurice glared. Borko looked around for Ace, to translate, and motioned him over. Borko mumbled something to

Ace, and Ace mumbled something in return. Borko announced, "No thief. Good boss, friend." He gave a bow and reached out his empty hand for a shake.

Maurice nodded, let go of the pen, and shook Borko's hand.

The men slapped Maurice's back, laughed, and slapped each other's backs.

Ace announced, "They say you good boss. They happy…you no smile. You mad, boss?"

Maurice sighed and stared at his pay. "Not mad, Ace. Sad. Disappointed. I spent all me savings last night. It was for Christmas gifts, and me family will go without. Josephine needs a new coat. That's the worst part. They depend on me ta feed them and…"

Ace frowned, "Bad." He spoke to Borko and the men. "Boss, they say, what you pay for whisky and girls?"

Maurice quoted the cost, and Ace translated.

Borko's jaw dropped. He yelled and gesticulated at the men. They yelled back and shoved each other until Borko punched a few men in their shoulders, and they nodded.

Ace chuckled. "Boss, Borko says they pay you some."

Maurice stared wide-eyed at them.

Borko grinned, slapped Maurice on the back, and yelled, "Good boss!"

Maurice invited Ace home with him for Christmas. He couldn't take all the men, because the homestead was a small, square box of a place. He planned to bring them some candy canes and some of Mary's cookies.

Biller pulled the wagon of gifts, including Josephine's new coat, and groceries from the store through the shallow snow.

"I learned somethin' new, Ace, I never would have guessed it. Being God's friend 'tis not a bore. He does some very strange things. I asked Him ta help me but didn't know if He'd answer. He showed me tools I had around me when I was in trouble. You must ask Him for yourself and see what He does."

Maurice slapped the reins, "Pick up the pace, boyo. Tis Christmas Day!"

His sisters spied Maurice and Ace from the kitchen window and ran out to meet them. Their red hair shone a stark contrast against the white background.

"Me heart only wanted a safe weapon, Ace." Maurice smiled and waved at the girls. "I also got respect and loyalty. Weapons don't need ta kill people, ya know. I asked God for one ta buy enough time."

Dalliance

Jan Verhoeff

"You may think you're lonely, but when I get done with you, you will know you don't understand the meaning of the word!" the screaming torments haunted her as she packed the last bag and loaded them into her car.

The year after high school, Megan left for college and a future of promise. She closed her eyes and remembered the winter ice storm; a car accident had stolen her mom and sister from her life. She fought tears as the struggle that followed their deaths surfaced again, leaving her feeling even more alone.

She pulled her arms tight around her waist and gave herself a hug, it was the best she could do to remedy that empty feeling she experienced whenever she thought of losing her family.

She remembered how Jeeve had come into her life that winter. He promised the moon and gave nothing. He took from her every ounce of sustenance she had to give and left her lonely, heartbroken and damaged.

She shook off the feelings of abandonment and struggled to fight her way through a moment of refilling the emptiness she'd felt during every moment spent with him. He sucked the life right out of her, leaving a hollow in the woman she'd been when they met.

This day, Megan captured a sliver of herself and took back a moment of time. Healing, just time enough to pack her bags and load them into her car. Escape from the torment was all she longed for. Yet, she knew there would be something more.

She silently vowed that she would not let Jeeve steal away her love, the city she'd dreamed of as a child, or the life she'd created for herself. But, for a time, she would escape him and return to the vast open world where she'd sprouted wings.

Megan Hawthorne had always traveled light. Few of the belongings in the home where she now lived belonged to her. A few mementos, her clothing, and the treasures of her heart lingered. She looked back for one last time, lifting the travel companion to her shoulder.

There was nothing more.

A single tear escaped the paled blue of her clear eyes and she swiped it away with the back of her hand. Another day disappeared into the night, and Megan closed the car door against memories that shook her core.

Love meant nothing, but it caused great pain.

The Denver city skyline faded into the mountains as she climbed the mesa to the east, steadily leaving the city behind. Home was a place she didn't want to go, but a place she knew would invigorate her dreams and lift her from the troubles of life. From the fading sunset in the western sky she felt darkness surround her, envelop her and suck all emotion from her body and soul.

Hours of riding the narrow black ribbon some called a highway led her to the deepest hollows of the prairie, a land that knew no mercy and revealed no kindness. When the darkness of night deepened, she stopped in the shelter of a small town park, to rest weary eyes. After a short nap, she awakened to colored lightning splintering the skies.

In the still of the night, she stepped out of the car for a moment to gain a fresh perspective on her location.

The distance she'd traveled had been short, only a few hours. Those hours seemed a lifetime behind her.

She sucked air into her lungs as she stepped out onto the shallow rise above the knob she'd known as a child to be home. No changes there. The savory aroma of sage still filled the air. Dank, damp dust, acrid and tainted with the smell of cattle in the valley surrounded her. She gazed into the dark moonless night and watched as lightning sparked behind heavy clouds, limped and pale in the darkness. She stood silent for a moment waiting for that feeling to wash over her.

It didn't come.

Slowly, she opened her eyes and gazed around. The incessant ding-ding of the car reminded her that her keys were in the ignition and her headlights were still on. The sound revoked in her mind the rapture she'd desired. She stood silent for one moment longer watching lightning play across the horizon before she folded and allowed her arms and face to hang limp toward the earth, relaxing and accepting energy the earth offered.

Standing once more she slid behind the wheel and drove deeper into the shadows. Slower, this time, with no haste. Dawn would be a long time coming and she wanted to arrive at the ranch as the sun rose over the buttes.

Black pavement faded to gray concrete, a highway created for prairie winters, high tech enough to keep the roads safe and hearty enough to last. She wondered at the wisdom, but accepted the value. Her car floated over the junctions, acknowledging each one with a near silent blip of the tires. The gentle whir of the engine lulled her into easy memories of long drives to the city with Pampa, and Noani.

She hovered on the edge of restlessness, dreaming of the past, stuck in the present, and experiencing the light show of the heavens in the distance. Her eyes closed for a moment and time stood still.

Megan opened gray eyes into the tranquil darkness. The depth of black she'd never seen before. Slowly she realized her car wasn't moving.

"Owe," she attempted to move her leg. She was trapped in the car. Asleep? She eased her foot away from the accelerator. She certainly wasn't moving. No lights in the car indicated the car was off. There was no sound from the engine, only the rushing sound of water. She looked around but didn't move.

Fear gripped every part of her as she felt the car rock precariously, as if high centered on something.

"Rushing water?" Her voice sounded muffled in the night air. She didn't remember rolling down a window. The chill air of the night slapped at her and she realized the window was broken.

"Don't move…" the voice from the darkness sounded familiar, but she couldn't see anyone.

"My car?" she spoke.

"Just sit still. I can't see what's holding you."

Thunder rumbled low, a growl in the distance, and the night drifted. Morning dawned with feathered ripples of light splintering through the clouds gathered on the horizon. Shallow ridges of color escaped, highlighting puffs of gray with pale translucent color and great swells of moisture gathered in the air. A promise of something greater, not yet arriving, the impression of what would come, hung on assurance.

Faded by the death of winter, sage brush sparked to life with the hint of spring, rays of sunlight glinted off dew drops, hastening the morning. The stirring of a new day began with a coyote drearily returning to his den. Another night of hunting done, he's hungry and alone.

In the stillness a rabbit rises from the shallows and crosses to a thistle for cover, too late. The coyote drags his prey a hundred yards or less and settles to dine.

Rain drops fall and the torrents flow, a rush of water gushes down the creek, through the draws, toward the river. Lightning flashes and thunder booms, echoing through the valley. Gullies wash between the roots of sage on the high prairie, and gulches form along the edges of mesas.

Streams of water erode and destroy, but moisture replenishes the earth.

"The tempest rides," Eva James looks out the oil paper window toward the eastern skies, "no sunlight today, we will live by the lamp."

She turned the oil soaked wick up a bit to light a lantern and watched the gentle glow fill the room. "Dalliance," she whispered. A moment of recognition danced about the room.

Eva pulled her shawl close and tucked more wood into the oven, stirring the embers of the night fire until they flickered to life. "Tel James, those calves are calling you." She gave her son a light shake and he opened his eyes, "they're just as cold as you are, and they're hungry too. Give them some grain and I'll have breakfast ready when you get back."

Tel slid his feet to the floor and stood up to his full height, pulling on a knitted sweater and his heavy winter pants. He pulled an overcoat on over the top and ducked through the pouring rain to run across the mud to the barn.

"Clara Evaline, greet the morning." Eva called jubilantly as she set the teapot on the potbellied stove in the middle of the room. "We've got breakfast to cook." Her sing-song voice and the melody she hummed as she worked around the heavy old table on the dining side of the room, blended with the pitter pattering rain pouring onto the metal roof.

Megan opened her eyes to a narrow squint and looked around the room that smelled of lantern oil and steeping mint leaf tea. The aroma of burning wood hit her and she snuggled under the covers. She didn't recognize the woman standing near the stove turning bacon in a cast iron skillet, nor the sod hut. She closed her eyes tight and blinked.

"Clara Evaline, it's morning... rise and shine." The woman spoke again and Megan realized she was looking straight at her.

"Um, what?" she gasped, stifling a yawn.

"Get your lazy bones out of that bed, girl. We've got quilting to do," the woman smiled at her, with sparkling eyes, and perfect teeth.

"Okay." Megan stretched and yawned again, taking a moment to look around.

The clothes she wore didn't feel like her silky night gown, or even her flannel pajamas, but they were warm. As she stepped out of bed, she found wooly slippers edged in fur with her toes, and looked around for clothes.

"Hurry up, Clara, Tel will be back in just a moment. You'd better be dressed! Else you'll have to hide behind the curtain."

The woman was talking to her, but what was that name she kept calling her?

Megan looked for her clothes and found a dark red patterned dress hanging from a hook at the head of the bed. Nothing else seemed to be hers. And that was the only dress around. She pulled it down from the hook and started to pull it over her night gown.

"Better take off that flannel gown, or your dress won't fit," the woman smiled at her, that delightful twinkle in her eyes again.

"Oh?" Megan laughed nervously, "yeah." She lifted the flannel gown over her head and found she was wearing a white muslin slip underneath. She pulled the red patterned dress over her head and the woman stepped forward to fasten it.

"Well, turn around here, girl. I can't reach behind you." She laughed a kind of jingling laughter that filled the room up with happiness.

"You'll need that sweater we knitted last winter. It's a mite chilly still."

"Yes," Megan tried to play along. "Where did I put that?"

"In the dresser, second drawer," the woman hummed a few notes of some long forgotten song, and danced her way back to the cook stove to turn the bacon. "Don't tell me you've done forgotten where we put things?"

"Just some things…" Megan admitted. "Is that mint tea?"

"Yes, of course, would you like cream in yours?" she poured another cup from the china teapot on the table. "Clara, you look mighty pretty in that sweater! I'm glad you chose that fresh pink color. It just looks ravishing on you!"

"Ravishing?" Megan fastened the top button and pulled it to fit around her slim figure. It felt warm, and she liked the soft pink color. The dark red dress under it had small pink flowers scattered over it. "It does go with my dress," she smiled at the woman.

Megan sipped at her tea and set it back on the table.

"I'm so glad to have you home. I know Mrs. Rockwell needs some help now and then, but I miss you so much when you're gone away. Tel and Papa just don't behave the same when it's just me here at the ranch," she took up the bacon and cracked five eggs into the pan. "One or two eggs?"

"Two please?" Megan realized she was ravenous. "I'm really hungry this morning."

Megan sipped her tea.

"Don't just stand there Clara Evaline, set the table. Tel and Pa will be back here any minute, now."

The woman took up the eggs and sliced off thick wedges of homemade wheat bread from the loaf above the stove. Megan looked around and found china on the sideboard to set the table, and silver in the drawer in one side of the table.

"Just one more silo of grain, Pa. Will we be selling those calves this spring?" Tel came through the door dripping water on the dirt floor. He took off his coat and hat, hung them on pegs by the front door. His boots came off and went on the mat just inside under the pegs. "These spring storms will bring up the wheat, but we can't plant corn in the mud."

"It'll dry, son." The older man nodded, hanging his coat and hat on the pegs and leaving his boots on the mat beside his son's. "Won't be long 'til we'll have more dry dust than we can breathe. Smells mighty fine in here, Eva Maureen."

"You just sit right down and I'll be pouring your tea, Jerrod," the twinkle in her eye got brighter.

Megan watched the interaction between them standing back near the sideboard.

"Clara Evaline, if you grow up half as perty as your mama, here, you're gonna be some looker!" He glanced her way and motioned toward the table. "Come on over here and sit down girl. It'll be nice to have your smiling face at the table again."

"According to Mrs. Rockwell, Clara Evaline can cook as good as Mama too, Pa." Tel straddled a chair and sat down across from Megan. "She says that Clara is one fine little homemaker, and she'll be right glad to get her back in the fall."

"Well, now, that's a nice report to have, but I'm just not sure our little Clara is available again this fall," the man nodded her direction.

Megan searched her memory for the name, Clara Evaline meant something, but she couldn't remember what it was.

"Please, pass the butter, Noani," Tel asked and looked straight at Megan.

"Noan... oh, yeah," Megan smiled at him and reached the saucer of butter across the table to him.

He winked and smiled back, "Thank you, Clara. You sure make the best butter."

She recognized his smile, but time seemed to have long passed. "Thank you, Tel."

"Of course, you remember, Clara, it's the cream from my heifer that makes the best butter." Tel knew.

"Of course, I remember. How could I forget that?" Megan answered, smiling now in recognition of the man, but not understanding the smooth boyish skin, the youth, and the vibrancy in his eyes.

"Only my Noani could make butter so wonderful with fresh cream, it didn't need sugar or salt for flavor," a glimpse of mischief sparkled in his eyes and she waited for more.

He had to give her more, but how did he know, when the others weren't aware. She looked at the woman who sat now at the end of the table and reached for her hand. They clasped hands and Megan shivered visibly. The touch sent a tremble through her that held her captive in the moment. She fought. She held onto the present, but the shiver quaked to her soul.

"Dear precious Lord, we thank you for this food. We're so glad to have our Noani back with us, we missed her so. Bless this day and these hands, this gathering and our work, in your precious name, Jesus, Amen." Tel said the prayer and Megan heard every word.

Megan looked around the room and realized the year must be 1931, but what was she doing here, and why did everyone believe she was her grandmother? And more important, she shuddered, what was that sense of foreboding that shivered through her when they clasped hands during the prayer?

"This is delicious!" Megan whispered, nibbling at the bacon and bread. She'd never eaten eggs blackened by an iron skillet before, but the flavor was good. The bread was a coarse texture but light and fresh.

"The food is always good." Pa said, "Your Ma's a great cook."

"Tel, you know who I am, don't you?" Megan leaned on the milk stanchion while Tel milked the cow he called his.

"Yes, Megan." His voice was more mature and he changed before her eyes. "Don't be frightened, but I have to be who I am, when I speak."

"What?" Megan stepped away from the older man whom she knew as her Uncle. "What's happening?"

"I'm not sure, what it is myself." He paused, realizing the cow was still waiting to be milked, he continued.

"You're Uncle Tel, Grandma's brother, right?" Megan looked at him, her eyes round and clear. "But you're living in both times." She shook her head slowly, "I don't understand?"

"Neither do I, and I don't know how you got back to this time. Or where Clara Evaline is right now?" He stood up, bringing the bucket of milk up with him. He moved the milk stool and reached to let the heifer lose.

"Do I really look like Noani?" Megan asked.

"Spitting image. I'd have never known if you hadn't been so confused about being here." He answered, "I don't think Ma and Pa know anything about you, or me."

He set the milk on the shelf and they fed the cows together. There were seven head in the barnyard, and three baby calves. He petted the two heifers and that came close and she noticed he walked with a limp.

"Uncle Tel, why am I here?"

"I don't know, Megan."

He looked at her straight, she knew she didn't have anything to fear, but she wasn't sure what her purpose there was. "Will I be able to go back?"

"I don't know," he answered, "I haven't figured out how I move though time. But if I'm talking to someone in this time, I am young, if I'm talking to you (from the future) I'm old. It's not so bad, I've gotten used to it. But you came back in time to an era when Noani was here. I guess, that's why everyone thinks you're her."

"But where is she?" Megan asked, looking around the area.

"I don't know. I suppose she could be in the future. She's never traveled forward, that I know of. But I suppose you changed places?" Tel shrugged.

"I was coming to see you." Megan explained. "I broke up with John Walker, it just wasn't working and I wanted to come home."

"You drove here?"

"Yes, last I remember I was crossing the Butte Creek Bridge. Then I was waking up and Ma was telling you to go feed the calves." Megan looked around, but her eyes stopped on the front door of the house, where Pa stood looking out at the barnyard. "Will he see you?"

"He only sees me in his time." Tel answered. "I don't know why."

"Interesting," Megan watched Tel change back to the young man her grandmother would have known. "What about the hands?"

"What do you mean?"

"When we held hands, during prayer, I felt a jolt like lightening." she explained, still wondering at that shocking jolt she'd experienced.

"I think it's the time thing. The only time I've ever traveled time is during a lightning storm. And it's frequently at night," he answered. "Then the first time I touch someone it's like a jolt of power escapes. I can't return for a while."

"Oh, is it just you?"

"I don't know. Jessica said once it's the Secret."

"Jessica?"

"You'll meet her here," he answered, a look of longing drifting over his eyes, and she remembered the name.

"Jessica? What year is this?"

"1931. Somehow, I always travel time about this time of year." He looked away at the sunset and watched the golden orb drop low behind the clouds. "Jessica is always part of those last moments, then she's gone."

"What do you mean?"

"The storm. I'm always here through the storm, and then I go back." Tel answered. "It's not the only time I travel, but it's the only time that's consistent."

"The storm?"

"It's coming. You'll know when it's here. Maybe we can get you back before it happens?" He looked hopeful. "I don't have any control over the time or travels."

"Oh…" Megan looked off in the distance, wondering.

Megan searched her mind for the history of 1931, she could barely remember stories of the dirt storms that crossed the prairies in the mid-thirties, before that, she kept drawing blank memories. Nothing seemed to fit.

As she listened to the night birds calling, everyone else slept. Megan stared out the oil paper window. The only glass windows in the old sod house were on the south walls, the eastern window above her bed was covered with smoky textured oil paper that kept out the rain, and prevented her from seeing anywhere.

Megan marveled each night at the starlight and the brilliance of each twinkling star. She loved the rich colors of the sky, and the radiance of the Milky-way, a cloud of stars that spanned the dark sky with such intensity that she could visualize the universe in bright array. Mornings brought dried mint tea, iron skillet blackened eggs, bacon from the slab, and fresh bread that Ma baked almost every day. Megan took her turn frequently, churning butter and making cheese in cloth lined bowls, pressing it hard to dry the curds and mold the cheese.

The work around the ranch was unending, but pleasant. She often heard Ma singing, humming tunes that grew familiar, or words that meant something from a different time. Megan wished for her keyboard to play, but kept silent except for an occasional tune she'd hum along if she recognized them.

As the gray light of dawn drifted through the oilcloth window, Megan drifted off to a dream filled sleep.

Noani gathered up her skirts and walked across the creek, wading ankle deep in the mud. Tel held up a child, and Megan waited to identify the child. She didn't know her name, but the child was happy and laughing in the sunlight. Time stood still on a summer afternoon, then Megan realized there was another person in the memory. Papa, she smiled in her sleep, the memory filling up the recesses of her mind and trudging on history, not yet created in this time from the past.

She remembered.

"Mama," Megan whispered, admiring the baby girl with golden curls. She fingered her own auburn curls and twirled them long, pulling the strands in longer coils. "Mama you were a pretty baby."

"Noani, we have to get the cattle." Tel called across the river, water rising around Noani's feet. "We have to go!"

Noani climbed into the wagon and took the baby. Tel drove, fast along the dirt road toward the darkening clouds in the west. Another storm. Megan tried to find the significance in the dream before she opened her eyes to Ma calling, "Noani, wake up dear."

"What?" Megan looked into the eyes of the woman with golden curls tied high above her forehead, falling low across the back of her head and wrapped in a loose coil near the nape of her neck. "Noani, you must wake up. It's morning," Ma spoke again, still lightly shaking her. "Tel has gone for the calves. We must prepare breakfast."

"Oh, yes," Megan stood up and grabbed her dress from the peg. She pulled the dress on, the flannel gown off, and tied the apron over the full skirt of her calf length dress. It seemed long for a girl, but Megan was probably shorter than Noani, who had been a rather tall woman.

"Ma, is there a creek nearby for wading?" Megan asked.

"In the summer you and Tel often go to the Mulberry Meadows." Ma answered and carried on with her work. "Have you forgotten?"

"Oh, no, I just had a dream, and it seemed so real. Noani, I mean, I was with Tel and we had a small girl with us. She was golden haired and we went to the creek." Megan explained.

"A small girl…" Ma looked up wistfully, "it's been so long since we had a child here."

"Why didn't you have more children, Ma?" Megan asked, looking at the woman's moist eyes.

"I couldn't have children, Noani. You and Tel were a blessing sent from Heaven. You just happened along. And we kept you. Angels brought you our way, and there was nobody to take you away." She whispered, as if it was a secret. "You were just a baby. Tel was almost two. The night you arrived on our door."

Ma rolled the yeast bread back and forth on the table kneading it into a smooth roll of dough. A tear rushed down her cheek and she wiped it away with the sleeve of her dress.

"I'd just done the wash and there were sheets on the line. I went to take them down and I heard a baby crying. I looked up and there he was, your Pa. At least, the man who had you in his arms. His face was damp from crying and he said, "I can't raise them alone, her mama died, and they're just too little for me to raise." He slid you into my arms and stepped off his horse." She stood quiet for a moment. "You can call her Clara Evaline, I named her for her mother, and you can add your name too. My boy is Tel. He placed you in my arms with a small bundle of clothes and swung Tel down off the saddle. When he mounted up again, I didn't realize I hadn't asked his name." She paused again. "When your Pa, my Frank came from town, I was sitting in the chair rocking you and he asked where I got you from." She wiped away a tear and put the bread in a bowl.

"I told him a man on a black stallion brought you, he must have been an angel. He gave me children." She rested for a moment, "I never knew his name. I've never known who he was, but he brought you and Tel to me, because he was alone and couldn't raise you."

"But you never knew who he was?" Megan asked, staring in awe at the story she'd just heard. "You're raising someone else's children?"

"No, baby Clara, you've never been someone else's children." Ma touched Megan's face and pulled her close, "Always mine, child. Always my baby girl. I've always loved you, and no mother could love you more."

"That is just... incredible! Unbelievable." Megan exclaimed. "You've never seen him since?"

"Not really." She answered.

"What do you mean?"

"Sometimes, I think he's watching."

"Like a guardian angel?" Megan offered.

"No, like I think he's somewhere around, watching you. I think he's nearby, watching you. Like he comes and goes, to see what you've become?"

"Eww! That's just creepy!" Megan shivered.

"Pa's seen hoof prints, where there ought'nt to be any." Ma spoke softly.

"Did you ever wonder? Do you want to know who he was?" Megan asked, watching the flickering lamp play at the flames, reflecting in the clear globe protecting it from wind.

The lamp flickered and Ma trimmed the wick. A low rumble came from high in the clouds outside the door, and Megan heard Tel in the distance whistling. She knew he'd be looking at the clouds. The storm was coming. She could feel it in the air.

Breakfast was always a big meal, little talk of anything that mattered much, but plenty of food. Pa said the blessing every morning and there were no more jolting shocks.

"The rain is gone," Tel spoke from the darkness on the eastern side of the house. She could tell without looking that he was Uncle Tel, not the boy she'd seen most of the day. "It's nice just to enjoy an evening."

"Yes, it's a beautiful evening." Megan peered through the darkness. "What's different?"

"Don't you feel it?" Tel joined her on the step. "It's as if time stands still?"

"I feel something, I thought it was the storm." Megan hedged, trying to understand the perceptions she experienced when Tel came near her.

She had no fear, he wasn't a threat to her.

The time they traveled held her still in this moment.

She didn't know.

She had no need to understand.

"Dalliance," he whispered.

"Dalliance?"

"The storm. The stallion. It's time. Dalliance."

Grizzly Escape

John Davis

Bold steps carried him from the mountain in a rushing walk, increasing speed as the elevation dropped. Darius wrestled his pack to the oversized rock near the water and dropped belly flat on the sand near the base of the path. He'd seen better days, but he would survive this one, too.

Face down, he washed the crusted blood from his neck and shoulder, allowing the cold to seep through him, easing the pain. Most didn't survive a run in with a Grizzly, but most were not Darius Glover, Lone Hunter of the North Woods.

Darius quickly wrapped the wounded shoulder in a clean white cloth, and pulled a sleeping bag from his pack. Exhaustion along with the pain of fighting the bear was quickly taking a toll.

He needed rest before he could make his way further down the mountain. And he had to sleep before dark. The bear might try to follow him in the dark. He slithered into the bag and closed his eyes.

The night birds sang, and crickets chirped. Darius struggled to awaken, but he felt suffocated, hot, and sweaty. He struggled, but he slept. Feverish, he awakened in the darkness, looked about and let his eyes adjust to the stillness. Trembling, he unzipped the bag and rose to a seated position on the rock. He could hear the water rippling along the creek behind him, and he felt a sense of peace surrounding him.

Night in the Rocky Mountains could be blissfully sweet.

He hadn't set up his tent. With the use of only one arm, it would have been a hopeless mess. Now, he rolled his sleeping bag, tied it on the pack and lifted the pack onto his back.

It had to be looped over his sore shoulder, to carry it, and he cringed as he seated the strap over the shoulder. His pain unrelenting.

The water sounded close and he remembered it being near the rock. But he didn't take time to search for water, he had to get moving. He turned on the headlamp and moved along the trail. It was an easy walk to the nearest highway, and someone would be passing by. He needed people. He needed medical care.

He walked.

Along the trail he found a few wild animals, but nothing that wanted to eat him. Mostly deer, raccoon, a porcupine nibbling at the remains of something, and the sounds of birds in the trees.

He walked.

He kept determinedly putting one foot in front of the other, intentionally not counting his steps. He didn't want to know how far he'd come, he just wanted to get there. He struggled to take each step.

He kept walking.

Near the base of the trail, he heard traffic, the drone of a truck somewhere below. He kept walking.

The adrenaline of the battle had dropped and his energy lagged. Darius knew he had to get somewhere, so he could get help. He kept walking. By the time he reached the highway, the sound of traffic was gone. He stood on the side of the road, leaning against the railing and waited. He'd walked along the highway until he arrived at a pull out and stood there, waiting. He'd pulled a white shirt from his pack, hoping to be seen by a traveler if he waved the shirt. He waited.

Before long he heard another truck coming and started waving the shirt with his good arm. He waved it until he heard the truck slow.

Walking toward the truck he heard the driver say, "Climb in!"

Inside the cab, he quickly said, "I was attacked by a grizzly. I need a hospital."

The driver answered, but Darius didn't hear him. He had passed out on the seat from the struggle to get into the cab. Feverish, he slumped in the seat against his pack, and the trucker drove.'

Darius awakened in the hospital hours later. The room painted a soft gold color, the window covered in slatted blinds with just enough light seeping through to tell him morning had arrived.

The delirium passed. He could feel the pain killers working. He was groggy, warm but not feverish. The sound of hospital equipment and the feel of blood pressure machines sent a chill through him. He dozed momentarily, then awakened to push the call button. He needed information.

The nurse arrived in his room, followed by a man in a dark green uniform. Department of Wildlife, Darius expected him.

Location. What was the grizzly? Why did he attack? All the usual questions. And Darius answered.

The grizzly would be on the hunt. He'd tasted human blood. He wasn't going to disappear into the mountains now. He would be looking for campers, innocents.

Darius knew the drill. But this was his Grizzly. He wanted to be the one to take him down.

He paused the conversation long enough to ask the nurse how long he'd be in the hospital.

Three days. He considered how long before the grizzly would begin to find his prey. Could it wait? Would he have time to get back to the hunt? He considered the wait… The time… The danger.

Is the possibility worth it? He wondered as he talked to the ranger, discussing options, and where the grizzly might be found.

He hadn't given the ranger enough information to find the grizzly yet, when he left. Darius wanted to talk to the Dr. first, before giving him more. He claimed exhaustion and asked if he could come back later. The ranger had walked out, looking back over his shoulder.

Darius closed his eyes and feigned sleep.

When the Doctor entered his room a few minutes later, he pretended to be resting while he listened to him discuss his condition with the nurse. When he touched Darius' shoulder, the Doctor remarked at the ease with which Darius continued to move his arm. The claw marks had been deep, but his muscles were still connected, and they would heal. The infection appeared to be minimal, and the meds had reduced his fever.

"How long will I be in the hospital, Doc?" Darius interrupted.

"Not long, another day. We want to make sure the infection is gone. You'll be taking pills for a while, and you're gonna need time to heal up." The Doctor explained. "Your muscles are good, they'll heal."

"Can I go back to the mountain?" Darius asked.

"For what?" The Doctor looked aghast at him.

"I live up there." He answered, "I don't have any place else to live."

"Well, I'd stay in town until the shoulder is healed. Then, it's up to you." The Doctor answered, "Make sure they find that bear and end him before you go back."

Darius nodded and rolled to the other side again, drifting off to sleep. He had all the answer he needed.

He would wait, and put that grizzly down himself.

The Whisker Dilemma

Jan Verhoeff

"Wild rabbits multiply like... rabbits." Carrigan announced on the 7 PM News, "Meanwhile vehicles left in the secured parking garage at the airport have wires and other various damage from rabbits eating the cover off during whatever time they're parked. Customers are up in arms, raging over the cost of repairs and damage to their vehicles. Airport officials have stated there is nothing that can be done about the damage and cost of repairs. What will happen now?"

Broker Winthrop listened to the media howl about the rabbits and wondered what could be done. His feet were propped on the coffee table and he continued eating his dinner, cold pizza from Reuben's, left over from the night before. He'd heard the uproar at the airport the day before as passengers were forced to call for tow trucks to remove their vehicles from the parking garage furthest from the gates. There had been threats and loud conversations when customers met with security guards about their cars not starting after only a few days in the parking garage.

Broker swept the trash from the parking areas; he'd seen the rabbit trails, watched them grow more and more abundant and wondered if something should be done. But his job was to manage the grounds, not take care of pests.

He kept quiet.

Inside the airport compound, rabbits were the top of the food chain. No coyotes, or other wild animals were small enough to get into the compound, so of course, rabbits were plentiful. Broker nodded his head in agreement with his own conclusion and changed the channel. He hadn't watched the Kardashians in several weeks.

Broker whistled as he walked from the employee parking lot to the office where he'd punch the time clock. Everyone always knew he was coming from half a mile away. His boss often joked that she knew if he was on the grounds, she could hear him whistling over the plane engines. He grinned at the thought, he liked Maggie. She was a good boss.

The yellow note on his time card said, "Meeting in the office 9 AM. Be there." He pulled off the sticky tab and put the time card back in the slot. He hated meetings, never had been good at presenting himself in front of others. He much preferred working the grounds, out near the fence where folks didn't know he was there, 'cept they could hear him whistle.

Broker looked at the watch on his left wrist and tucked the note in his pocket. He had work to do and not much time to do it, if he had to appear at some meeting. He whistled some long, low tune as he walked toward the exit.

"Broker?" Maggie was sitting behind her desk with the door open. He heard her call his name before he got to the door.

"Yeah?" He stood in the doorway to her office.

"You got the note?" She asked.

"Wha'do they want with me?" He took the ball cap off his head, smoothed down the imaginary hair that had long since disappeared from the top of his head and put the cap back in place.

"Actually," Maggie stood up and walked around the desk. Her skirt was hiked up over her knees and she let it fall, a narrow black sheath, crimped in at a narrow waist, topped by a shiny red blouse that draped across her ample bosom, layered with gold chains and a tassel that hung between them. He watched her pull her long dark curls back away from her face and waited patiently for her to continue speaking. "I need you to come up with a solution for those darned rabbits that doesn't include shooting them. That'd be my preference. I'd just call my brother and his buddies in with their shot guns and tell them to have at it."

"That's why you're all pertied up? They want you to talk?" He asked, ignoring her request.

"Well, technically…" She leaned on the desk, crossed her feet at the ankles and folded her arms in front of her, "They want you to offer a solution. You're the yard manager. I just dressed up to give you some clout and support." She grinned.

"Imp!"

She poked her tongue out at him and returned to her chair, behind the desk, "Have a seat." She motioned to the leather covered chair in front of the desk, one of two matching chairs moved in from someone else's office, to make her office look like a power lounge. "Any ideas?"

"Dogs. Hounds. They like to eat rabbit, and they'll hunt anything." He shrugged and sat down, "I got three of 'em, Jack's got three, and I probably can find more'n that if I ask around. They'll each eat about a rabbit a day if we let 'em out there."

"So, we could start within a week or so?" She asked, "You think we could clear out a hundred or so within the month?"

"N'yeah, we could most likely empty out a hundred rabbits in a month, if I bring 'em out every day or so. We could do that…" He nodded.

"Do you want to propose that? Or shall I?"

"I'll watch ya…" Broker nodded, chewing the inside of his lower lip.

"Ha. Ha." She picked up a note pad and started writing.

Broker left the office and spent the next several minutes sorting tools in the work room near the exit. The meeting would happen soon enough, he didn't need to sit and worry for time to get there.

Seven people sat in the big conference room in the front hall of the office end of the airport, three women and four men. Broker followed Maggie into the room and sat to her left. On his left was a small woman with long blonde hair, wearing pink. Broker didn't notice much beyond the color of her clothing; it wasn't the strong bold colors Maggie chose. Pink, the kind of pink that one might imagine a baby's cheeks to be a few hours after birth, and she sat right beside him. Broker had a hard time focusing on any part of the conversation in the meeting. He never said a word. When Maggie spoke, he tried to listen. But he really never heard a word. His attention was totally consumed by the pink lady beside him. Even when she spoke, he heard nothing.

When Maggie asked him to explain the dog solution, he stumbled over the words, but explained in a minimum of seconds that the dogs would hunt rabbits, and within about a month, they could reduce the population by about a hundred rabbits. A long slow sigh went around the room and the lady in pink responded… "Why don't we just feed the rabbits so they're not hungry enough to eat the wire?"

The end of the meeting had included one disagreement after another, nobody agreeing to anything, until two of the women and two of the men left. One woman had said she didn't think they'd find any solutions for the rabbit problem. The lady in pink had been nearly in tears, but Broker didn't understand why she was crying. He just felt bad that she left in such a rush.

The woman who remained was an executive with the Parking Garage Council and she agreed with Maggie that the rabbits would need to be exterminated. Her solution included poison.

There had been a huge fuss over that, and ultimately, Broker understood that Maggie's solution would be the first attempt made to rid the airport of pesky rabbits.

Long after she was gone, if Broker leaned a little to the left, he could still smell the sweetness of the lady in pink. He was pretty much oblivious to anything else.

Broker followed Maggie to her office. The pink lady had returned to her gate and boarded a plane headed for some far distant destination and Broker wished he'd paid more attention. He didn't know where she came from, or if he'd see her again. Maggie seemed upset with him when she told him he could contact Jack and they could bring in the dogs the following Saturday morning.

Broker didn't whistle as he worked. He worried that he hadn't made any impression on the Pink Lady, and now it was too late.

The dogs were waiting when he got home, and he fed them first. He considered their next meal. Rabbit? It could be. He considered... Perhaps, he could take three dogs the next morning and see what might happen when he set them loose near the outside fence. He fed them a light meal and sent them to their beds. He wanted them well rested and a little hungry the next morning. His own meal was a lightly grilled steak, medium well with a side of bread and butter.

Daybreak wouldn't happen for another twenty minutes. Plenty of time for him to load the dogs and drive to the airport, and the rabbits would still be out foraging for food. He settled behind the wheel and drove ten miles across the back road to the entrance. He parked in the outside open parking far away from the cars. Getting out of the vehicle, he spotted seven good sized rabbits, and a few smaller ones. He heard a low growl from his hunting hounds in the back, before he unlatched their cages. Within minutes, each had brought back a rabbit.

He loaded them into their cages, with the rabbit carcasses and let them eat as he drove home. The snarling, growls of happy, contented dogs filled the back of his truck. It wasn't Saturday. Jack hadn't come with him. But they were three rabbits down.

The work day started almost two hours later. Broker went to BeGee's for breakfast. Jack met him and they talked about Saturday.

Two days away.

Broker explained how it worked that morning, and Jack agreed, it would be best to do the hunt at daybreak. The earlier, the better.

Seven trucks with dog cages arrived at the airport Saturday morning. The hunt club gathered toward the outer edge of the employee parking lot and unloaded their dogs. Each hunter took his dogs on leashes to the outer edge of the area and turned them loose. Within an hour, nineteen dogs, each with a rabbit carcass loaded up and pulled out of the parking lot, snarling contentment as they ate their fill of something that didn't have feathers.

On the calendar, Broker noted "19" and circled the number.

Each morning for the next two weeks, Broker and however many hunters could participate, showed up with dogs for a morning hunt. Each morning, Broker wrote a number on the calendar and circled it when he punched the time clock.

On the last day of the month, Broker awakened early to the patter of rain drops on the roof. He blinked, rolled over and went back to sleep. No reason to load the dogs if it were raining, he slept until the alarm went off and dressed for work. With the rain stopping, he decided to try just three dogs. By the time he arrived at the airport, the roads were dry, but the grassy plains would still be damp. He wondered if the rabbits would be out, or if they'd be hidden in warm holes, holding out for dry weather.

Jack and three other hunters joined him in the parking lot. They unloaded their dogs and walked across the buffalo grass to a fence where they hadn't hunted before. Broker heard the Gator shift gears, but didn't look back to see who was coming his way. Security guards had known he was there several mornings, but hadn't bothered him. He figured it was time one of them came around to check him out.

Dreary low hanging gray clouds smothered out the sound of a shrieking woman. The dogs, trained on their prey, tugged at the leashes.

"Don't turn them loose!" The shrieking woman spoke too late. Broker had released the third dog.

"Sorry, they're off…" He answered, looking up for the first time to recognize the blonde haired woman who had worn pink for the meeting. This time she was dressed in white capris, sparkling slippers and a fluttery butterfly blouse with many colors, her long blonde hair blowing in the breeze.

"Call them back!" She demanded.

"Mr. Winthrop, there's a meeting at the airport. Ms. Hansen has brought in a team of animal behavior experts and she's got a warrant to stop the abuse of the rabbits." Mr. Shaffer, an executive from the airport spoke in a husky voice.

Broker ignored him. The dogs had already caught their rabbits and were headed back to the truck.

"Mr. Winthrop, I order you to contain those monsters. They're hurting the bunnies!" Tia Hansen shrieked again.

"Ms. Hansen, the bunnies are dead." Broker followed the dogs to the back of his truck, a few yards away and latched each cage as the dogs climbed inside.

"Mr. uh… Broker… this isn't going… This isn't … going a… as … well … as…. I really expected this… to happen a … little…. Uh… differently." Mr. Shaffer stumbled over the words. He was obviously shaken by the site of the dogs eating the rabbits.

"I have warrants. I'm not happy, Mr. Winthrop." Tia screeched. "From the moment I heard you'd started hunting the rabbits, I knew this was going to be trouble. I told you NOT to do this, but nobody listened. Now, I've been forced to obtain warrants and there will be arrests made."

Broker glanced at the security guard driving the John Deere green Gator and shrugged, "I suppose if you must, Ms. I was just doing my job."

"Mr. Winth... Broker, you'll meet me in the conference room in ten minutes." Mr. Shaffer commanded.

"The uh... Dogs. I have to take them home," Broker started to explain.

"They'll have to wait," Mr. Shaffer looked away.

Broker looked at the dogs and then across the parking area as other hunters loaded their dogs. He waved to Jack and pointed toward his dogs. Jack nodded, latched his last dog and moved his truck closer to Broker's. Jack raised a hand, signaling that every dog got a kill. The numbers were rising.

After Broker and the others had left, Jack loaded Broker's dogs in his truck and drove away from the airport.

Maggie seated herself next to Broker in the conference room, her hand on his shoulder offered assurance, but she wasn't sure he'd need it as much as she had. She'd taken full responsibility for the hunt and told him to bring the dogs. If anyone's head was on the chopping block with Shaffer, it would most likely be hers. Broker fumbled with a pencil in front of him, sometimes drawing scrolls or a scrawl on the note pad. He looked like a fish out of water in this room with high powered executives. Maggie paid no mind to the fact that she was dressed in jeans and a blue work shirt for this meeting, after she'd taken pains in the last meeting to upgrade her professional appearance; she hadn't had any warning for this one.

Shaffer looked like he'd seen a ghost, or dead rabbits. Maggie grinned inwardly at the thought of Shaffer watching dogs eat rabbits. She'd noted that he rarely even looked at the meat counter in the cafeteria. His tastes ran to the garden variety counter and salad bar. *No wonder he identified with the burrowing bunnies.*

Tia Hansen had been going off at her assistant since Maggie walked in the room, in tones that everyone could hear, though her words were too muddled to understand. Maggie wondered if he understood her.

"This meeting was called because Ms. Hansen has warrants intended to stop the murder of the rabbits on the site." Shaffer spat out the distasteful words, "I'll call it to order and invite Ms. Hansen to speak for herself."

Shaffer wiggled his way into his seat and left Ms. Hansen standing near the head of the table.

"I was notified last week, by Mr. Shaffer, that the staff at the airport continued with their plan to have dogs kill the rabbits. I find such actions distasteful and barbaric. Not only are these actions barbaric, but they are against the law. I've brought these documents ordering you to cease and desist, and expect such practices to stop immediately. I am determined to prevent the deaths of any more innocent bunnies. I am prepared to file warrants for the arrest of anyone who ignores these orders." Tia Hansen passed out copies of the legal document she'd brought with her.

Maggie scanned the document, standing, "This is nothing more than a complaint filed with the courts. What right do you have to file a complaint action against the airport? These rabbits are costing us thousands of dollars in damages and liability claims from customers parked in our garages when their vehicles are damaged. We have to protect our customers. The rabbits are pests that must be eliminated. That's our job." Maggie looked around the table at other airport employees for support, and sat down when she found none.

"They are animals on your grounds and you are responsible to feed them, not kill them," Tia argued. "They're hungry. If you feed them, they won't be eating the wires."

"They're wild rabbits. There are acres of grass out there on the prairie to eat, instead, they find their way into the parking lots and garages and eat the covering off the wires of parked cars." Broker explained, frustration showing in his voice, "Ms. Hansen, what would you suggest we do, provide bunny protectors and have them carry your precious wild rodents back to the prairie and show them the grass?"

"If necessary, yes, you need to hire animal control officers to take the bunnies back to a safe area. Then feed them, so they'll stay there." She expounded, "Perhaps if you planted carrots and lettuce for them outside the parking areas, they would be more content?"

"This is an airport! You want us to provide the bunnies with a garden?" Broker was outraged.

"If not here, then catch them and put them out in to the wild where they can find enough food." Tia shrieked. She stamped her foot for impact and sat down. The pout on her face had little impact on Broker.

"Would you be available to spend your time capturing their tiny little hearts, and carrying them to safety in the big woods where coyotes, wolves and wild cats won't dare to eat them?" His words dripped sarcasm.

"Now, now. Mr. Winthrop, this is an option. If we set some traps with food in them, we could possibly catch the bunnies and remove them to another location," Mr. Shaffer admonished.

Broker didn't respond.

Maggie let a sigh escape her lips and started to speak. Mr. Shaffer cut her off.

"I'm certain there would be volunteers from PETA to help with the relocation process, Ms. Hansen?" he asked.

Broker shifted uneasily in his chair and Maggie glance at him, measuring the situation before she spoke again, "I don't know that we would be able to relocate so many rabbits safely. Mr. Shaffer, you know we're already having a problem of sorts along these lines."

Maggie's implication didn't go unnoticed, although Broker didn't understand what she meant. Shaffer raised an eyebrow and kept quiet. Maggie was pretty certain Shaffer knew Broker was unaware of their quarantine problem.

"Why not? Boulder removed their prairie dog population to Southeast Colorado a few years back, the farmers and ranchers appreciated the new targets. I'm certain they'd appreciate a mass of new jack rabbits for rabbit stew." Broker's voice was harsh, almost scathing, "The point is, whether we kill them here, on the compound, or they're killed in the wild, the bunnies – er… Jack Rabbits – are going to die."

"We still have the option of poisoning the rabbits," an executive from the airport security announced. His demeanor implied he knew something about the project, Maggie noted.

"No. Absolutely not. That is an unacceptable method of removing the rabbits from the airport grounds!" Tia exclaimed. "You will not poison the rabbits on my watch."

Maggie watched the frenzy erupt before her eyes and wondered if she'd be able to bring the volume down on any level. Broker sat quietly beside her, his voice had been heard and he was done. Maggie wondered if this was going to be a major problem for much longer, but knew she was losing control of the situation, whatever turn it might take.

Broker followed Maggie to her office and stood in silence as she opened the door. He didn't speak. His presence was enough. She entered and closed the door.

Five days later, Broker tallied up the number on the calendar. Two hundred, and fifty-eight rabbits were dead. He looked around the airport parking garage and couldn't tell they'd even made a dent in the number of rabbits lurking in corners, eating wires and huddling against the walls of the parking garage. If anything, there seemed to be more. He stopped at Maggie's office on his way to lunch.

"Has there been any real reduction in damage?"

"The numbers are down, but not by much. Why?" She asked.

"I counted up the totals. More than two hundred and fifty dead and I can't tell we've even put a dent in the number of rabbits in the garage. We'll have to somehow run them out of the garages, to get the numbers down." He answered, selecting a variety of greens from the buffet. He topped the salad with a large helping of grilled chicken and dumped on salad dressing.

"That stuff will kill you!" Maggie dipped a small amount of dressing onto her salad.

"That's what you've been telling me for four years." He answered, grabbing a large dip of bacon to throw on top.

"So… Why are we not eliminating rabbits?" Maggie sat down at a corner table and left the open side for Broker.

He sat down and considered the question. He didn't have an answer, at least not an answer that he wanted to voice out loud. He had wondered about another issue, but it seemed more like a conspiracy theory, and he most definitely wasn't into that crap. He focused on stirring the salad dressing into his salad, while Maggie continued to voice her opinion on the rabbits. He listened, without commenting.

"Did we ever have a count on those critters?" Maggie focused on her own salad. Her thoughts obviously far away, "It just seems there were so many, and now… Well, I just can't tell any are gone. Maybe more in the garages. It's as if…" Maggie looked off into the distance, as if she could see through walls. "No, I can't imagine how that could happen."

Broker sat back in his chair and folded his arms. "Spill it?"

Maggie shrugged and took a few bites of her salad. She chewed rabbit food while Broker watched. When her phone rang, Broker thought she looked relieved.

He wasn't comfortable with her silence, or her words. He struggled more when she excused herself and took her tray and the call back to her office.

Broker pushed his own salad around on the platter, nibbled a bit at the bacon and emptied his glass of watered down cola. He took the last drink and dumped his own half-eaten platter of food, before moving back toward Maggie's office. By the time he arrived, the door was closed and he could hear voices inside. He had work to get done.

Broker punched off the time clock at 4:30 as dark clouds rolled over the prairie. Rain, blessed sweet drops of heavenly tears would sprinkle the land and water the buffalo grass. He walked to his truck as the first drops splattered the ground. Lightning flashed across the sky. Thunder rumbled and rolled, then crashed like an ocean wave to the shore. He started the truck and pulled out onto the highway headed for home. He was exhausted, but the further he drove, the more he wanted to turn back.

At the first junction, he realized he'd made the turn, headed back for the airport. He didn't pull into the employee parking, but instead drove through the departure lanes, into the covered parking. He drove through layer after layer of the covered parking, noting the rabbits huddled in the corners of the garage shivering and cold. In some places he counted as many as ten rabbits along a shallow wall. Other places, there were rabbits hopping out of his way as he drove down the lane, between parked cars.

As he drove down the last lane, he noticed rabbits near the ramp. They didn't seem to be interested in moving out of his way, and one hopped right into the side of his truck. He felt a thud as it rolled beneath him. The dead thud of an animal dying gave him no satisfaction. This animal would not be food for the circle of life. Broker drove into the drenching rain and followed the road into the city. He was going home.

Dover, his oldest hunting hound howled as he left his truck. Broker fed the dogs and settled in front of the television with a beer. He wasn't hungry.

Broker fell asleep in his chair, watching a documentary. He wasn't interested in anything being said, but it was noise that kept him from thinking about the pretty girl in pink and how desperately he wished she wasn't disagreeing with everything he said at the airport. He drifted off, dozing against the pillowed cover of his chair.

Sunlight streamed through the east window of Broker's apartment, waking him up more than twenty minutes after he should have been leaving for work. He stumbled out of the chair and rushed through his morning routine. Shower, shave, dress and feed the dogs, he slid behind the wheel of his truck and sped toward the airport, watching for the local police. He didn't need a ticket.

Inside the gates, he took the back road to the employee parking, slowing along the way as he noticed dead rabbits on the road. More dead rabbits filled the parking lot, and even more along the walls of the parking garage.

"Shaffer, I don't give a rat's patutti in Hades if you bought the poison or not. You threatened to poison the rabbits and they're dead. I'm holding you personally responsible for the brutal and unnecessary murder of the rabbits on the airport grounds. And I will see your arse in court!" Tia Hansen stomped out of Maggie's office as Broker punched the time clock. Her heels clicked a bold rhythm on the tile floor as she walked toward the main part of the airport. Her assistant half ran to keep up.

Inside the office, deadly silence was disrupted by the ringing of a phone. Maggie answered. Shaffer sat stone faced across the desk from her, listening as Maggie edged her way out of a press interview, offering to let the reporter in on any information she had as soon as she had anything to tell. Broker walked in, sat down in the third chair and shut the door behind him.

When Maggie hung up the phone, she buried her face in her hands and let out a long slow sigh. Broker recognized the furious tone she attempted to hide. He allowed his brows to knit together as he watched her, wondering what could be the cause of her frustration.

"Broker, when you couldn't bring the dogs anymore, did you take other action?" Maggie's question caught him off guard. He'd spent most of the spare time he'd had over the past few days in her presence. She should have known he'd taken no other action.

"Maggie, I've been with you. How would I have possibly taken any other action?" He asked quietly, trying to understand what he was being accused of.

"You've had some time, and you drove through the parking lots last night, just before we noticed the rabbits were dying. We have you on video." Shaffer asserted.

"The rabbits are dying?" Broker asked. "What are you talking about?"

"Many rabbits, inside the covered garages. When I came to work this morning, there were literally dozens of rabbits dead just inside the gates, throughout the garages. They're almost all dead..." Shaffer asserted again. "Tia Hansen arrived at the same time we did and she's already working on warrants for your arrest, because we have you on tape."

"You have me driving through the garage, counting rabbits last night on my way home from work." Broker admitted, looking the both of them over, waiting for more response.

"We do have you on tape. You drove down almost every aisle of the garage last night. You really expect us to believe you were counting the rabbits?" Shaffer demanded. "You know there are cameras; you didn't expect to get caught poisoning the rabbits?"

"Wait. Hold everything? You think I poisoned the rabbits? Why would I go and do a thing like that? Once they're poisoned they're not food for the dogs. Anything that eats them is going to die and it's a vicious circle that never ends. I'd NEVER poison the rabbits. That was never my idea." Broker stood up and pushed away from the two of them. "I can't believe you'd even accuse me of such a thing."

"Broker, wait." Maggie stood up and walked around her desk, "I didn't accuse you of poisoning the rabbits. I know you'd never do that. But someone poisoned them. Or... something..."

She stared right at Shaffer and stood there waiting for him to say something.

"Maggie, if you know something, you'd better be letting it fall. Because accusing me of poisoning the rabbits isn't going to wash," Broker focused on her face and waited a moment.

"Shaffer, spill it. He needs to know…" Maggie spoke directly to Shaffer.

"It's top secret information and he hasn't got the clearance." Shaffer started.

"Somebody better start talking." Broker leaned hard against the door, "You two have had something going on for several days now, and I want to know what it is."

"About a week ago, we got a cargo plane in, with a load of animals. They came in from an area that had been quarantined during the time the flight was in the air from Africa, and there were several rabbits on board." Shaffer started, "They were young, caged and quarantined, and we had to keep them here at the airport until someone could pick them up from the quarantine shelter. They were picked up the second day by a representative of PETA. Before they got off the airport grounds, she and Tia met and they decided there was no reason to keep them all cooped up, when they could run free here on the airport grounds and they released them."

"Quarantined?" Broker looked at the two of them, "From what?"

"Bubonic Plague." Maggie answered.

"A week?" Broker looked back and forth between the two of them, "Have you called the health department?"

"Broker, it will shut down the airport!" Shaffer whined.

"So will the plague," He answered. "Call Tia and get her back here! NOW! Maggie, call her. She may be infected too."

Maggie picked up the phone and dialed. Shaffer tried to stop her, but Maggie gave him a warning look and Broker laid a hand on his shoulder. Nothing could stop them now. They had to get the word out.

"Shut down the flights. Shut the gates. Nobody leaves the airport, nobody comes in or out of the grounds. URGENT SECURITY ALERT. Close the gates." Maggie repeated the alert into the phone.

"How long have you known?" Broker asked.

"Shaffer heard them talking as they took the rabbits, that they wouldn't really have to take them off the grounds, they could let them loose on the grounds here." Maggie explained.

"I talked to Maggie a few minutes after, because she came into my office. There were fifty-seven rabbits, many of them pregnant females. The plane was scrubbed down in one of the bays and sent back to Africa." Shaffer kept talking as Maggie dialed the phone.

Within moments there were sirens and airport alerts, announcing that the airport was closing down for security reasons and everyone was to go to the main terminal security area. Maggie made more phone calls. Shaffer sat there, repeating his story, as if he had to hear it again himself.

Broker left the office, responding to Maggie's question that he'd be back. He walked toward the main hall of the terminal. He found Tia standing in the middle of the chaos, hundreds of people collecting in the center of the airport. She appeared lost in the crowd.

"What's going on?"

"You set the rabbits free, and they've infected the airport with the plague – my best guess." Broker answered.

"No, they were healthy rabbits. There was no reason to quarantine them." She answered, "People are just so mean, keeping them in those tiny cages. They needed to be free."

"They died, Tia. They infected the rabbits in the parking garages and they're all dying of the Bubonic Plague." Broker had pulled her away from the crowd and was trying to make her understand the devastation she'd caused.

"The rabbits, they were so scared, backed into the corner of their cages, like they were frightened. So scared. We just let them free so they could hop with the other rabbits. They were frightened." Tia cowered against the wall, crying.

"Let's go back to the office, Tia. Come with me," Broker led her back toward Maggie's office, through the maze of people, most of them going the other direction...

Access, Hash Browns, Cherry Pie
Heidi Kortman

Thump. Dennis Flannery swung forward on his crutches, planting his remaining foot at the edge of the top step. Behind him the door *clicked* closed. Nothing tugged at his back, so he'd managed to keep the tails of his overcoat from getting caught. *One good thing. Keep the list growing, like you teach your patients?*

The apartment he'd shared with an intern since his release from the rehab facility was musty and cluttered. Depression festooned its corners, cobwebbing his spirit. Not a place to recapture his purpose, or any different dream.

He set the crutches on the next step down, careful to avoid the crack in the cement. *I don't need two legs to battle childhood cancer.* He turned left at the bottom of the stoop. Circling the block from that direction would increase his stamina, or so he maintained, stifling the persistent mental mockery that yes, he feared negotiating the stretch of street where he'd been struck by the snow plow.

The trouble with the self-delusion was that soon his stump throbbed with each new landing. Two thirds of the distance down the block, his wet palms trembled on the crutch grips but hospital hallways were longer. "God, bless the kids on the ward. I can't be there, yet, to help."

His left crutch tip skidded on a paper scrap, and he fought for balance. "Pay attention. Don't fall now. They've scheduled you for a prosthetic fitting next week."

The trash collector ahead did an obvious double take. Dennis flinched. How loudly had he spoken?

He clomped on, and managed to reach the next corner.

A bus shelter stood a few yards past that, and backing against the cold aluminum, Dennis sagged onto one end of the bench. He stacked the crutches beside his right knee and turned his face toward pale spring sunshine.

Bus brakes hissed, and passengers descended. One paused, blocking the light. "Doctor Flanagan?"

Dennis opened his eyes. "Yes." *Kerry Post's mother.* "Mrs. Post. How's your boy?

The woman blotted her cheeks with her scarf. "After your accident, his case was transferred to Doctor Bell, who changed Kerry's chemo regimen. My son got so sick. He cried for you, and Doctor Bell wasn't comfortable praying with him when he asked."

"Wasn't." Dennis swallowed hard. "Has that improved?"

Mrs. Post sat beside him, and hid her face in her hands. "No." Her shoulders shook. "Kerry died last month."

My impulsive choice to jaywalk has harmed so many more than me, Lord. Please forgive me.

He cleared his throat. "I can't undo what happened..." His words came in a sorrow-thickened whisper.

"I'm on my way to my mother-in-law's." Kerry's mother shifted on the bench. "She wants to walk to the cemetery."

Dennis heaved himself upright, and awkwardly offered a handshake. "I'm fighting to get strong enough to work. Next week, they'll fit me with a trial prosthesis."

She stared at his outstretched hand. "I can't deny that's good news for you." She stood.

"Mrs. Post...I'm so sorry." *Useless words. I prescribed what I thought was best, but Bell's choice might have been more effective if her son could've withstood it.*

The woman's phone buzzed, and she glanced at it. "I'm late, Doctor Flanagan. Good bye." She stepped away with speed he'd probably never match again.

He shifted the crutches, knowing he couldn't stay there all day. Phantom pain stabbed as though he'd twisted his missing ankle and knee while sweat trickled between his shoulders.

A medication bottle rattled in his deep pocket as he swung forward, tempting him to take another dose, but he knew he had another three hours to endure. "Don't get dependent," he muttered.

How could he find a distraction from his anxiety and discom—? No! His state needed bald honesty—near-constant pain. Dennis paused. Retreat to the bus stop and ride? Nope. Not quitting.

Teeth clenched, he deliberately extended his stump from the hip, in an approximation of the motion the therapist had explained he'd need to make habit while using the pylon-like initial prosthesis.

Swing. Thump. Rattle. Repeat. Step-dancing it wasn't, but in another seven yards, he'd round the corner. Triumph in any size counted. "God, bless the kids on the ward."

Sunshine split the overcast, and he squinted. Items glinted on the sidewalk ahead as he moved closer.

"Loose change. Quite a bit of it." Three quarters, four dimes, one... no... two nickels. Not enough to buy much, but still worth picking up. Dennis stopped, and took time to check in every direction for lurkers.

From where he stood, gathering the quarters would be quickest and simplest. Shifting his right crutch into his left hand with the other, he bent and snatched them. The dimes, more scattered, forced him a couple of steps forward.

He'd closed his fingers on the third dime, when footsteps approached.

"Let me help you with that, Doc."

The voice was familiar. Dennis glanced to his left, as Bill Cluchie scraped together the last dime and the nickels. The beat cop dropped the coins into Dennis's palm.

"Thanks, Bill."

"Haven't seen you around for a while. I was beginning to think you'd moved out of town."

Don't I wish. "Nah, I'm still doing rehab. Just got back to the neighborhood." He glanced again at the coins before adding them to the pocket with the pill bottle.

"How much money'd you drop? Should I be looking for more?" Bill sidestepped, and scanned the gutter. "Nothing landed in there."

"I didn't drop the change."

Bill shrugged as his stomach rumbled. He chuckled. "My appetite knows I've been past Charlie's Diner. His pie-of-the-day is cherry. Soon as my shift is over, I'll take one home."

"Great idea." *Charlie's Diner.* "I haven't been there in... four months." *Might be the place to take my mind off the pills in my pocket.* "I think I'll head that direction."

Thump. Rattle. Clink. Dennis winced. *They'll hear me approaching from a block away.* He knew the sequence too well. First, a nervous glance, and then a grimacing double-take in reaction to his injury. He hadn't decided which of the following reactions was worse, the solicitousness, or put-on obliviousness that he surmised most hoped he'd interpret as tolerance, but was nothing but awkward.

He crutched forward, punched the crosswalk signal button, and counted the seconds under his breath as he scanned the asphalt, planning how to dodge the encroaching potholes.

Dennis swung through his first step, and reached out with the crutches to take another when a bicycle messenger *whizzed* past, not two feet away. He flinched, staggering.

Didn't even hear the chain in the derailleur. I've got to do better. His sweating palms slicked the crutch grips, and his breath came short. Get out of the street. A quick check for more traffic, and he forged ahead, to stand unscathed in the curb cut.

"Good morning!"

The greeting, from his left, kept him from a collision with an elderly man and a teen, both in wheelchairs. Dennis couldn't put names to their faces. "Good morning."

"I used to be one of the crazy cyclists in this neighborhood." The teen turned his neon-orange chair to face Dennis. "Now, I've got these four wheels instead of two, and I'd rather have a Mustang."

"Yeah. I had my eye on a Corvette." Dennis responded. "Where're you going?"

"To play basketball." The teen pulled a phone from his pocket. "Gotta go, or I'll be late. See ya, George." He rolled off.

The older man nodded.

That kid's coping. I can too. Dennis shifted a crutch forward.

"You new in the neighborhood? I'm George Sayer." The gentleman reached up, offering a handshake.

Dennis juggled his crutches, and gripped the broad, brown hand. "No, but I recently got released from a rehab center. Dennis Flannery."

George smoothed his soul patch with his index finger. "Hope you don't mind my sayin' this, but you look rough. You okay?"

Dennis switched his crutches to the other hand, gritting his teeth. That flaring phantom pain raised sweat beads on his forehead. He mopped them with his sleeve. "I've got pain pills in my pocket, but I can't take the next dose yet. I'm looking for a distraction."

"My grandson got hooked on his. Been fightin' 'em for six years now."

"He's managing to stay off?"

"Yeah, and I'm backin' him up with prayer all the time." George rolled his chair ahead.

Dennis swung onto the sidewalk, and the items in his pocket *rattled*. "What's his name? I'll add him to my list."

"He's Antony. Thanks. Glad to meet another man who keeps a list. Don't know why there aren't benches on this side of the block. Think you can keep goin' for another two?"

"We'll see. I'm building stamina so I can get back to work."

"Where's that?" George gestured forward because the walk was too narrow to move side-by-side.

Dennis got behind the chair. "Mass General. I'm a pediatric oncologist."

"Them's some long halls. Man, kids and cancer. Two words that oughtn't to ever go together." George shook his head, then spun his chair sideways. "So, you're Doc Dennis."

"Charlie called me that. So did my patients. How'd you know?"

"Come on, Dennis. You've got t'see this."

George sent his chair ahead with a powerful shove. Dennis *thumped* and *rattled* at a faster pace than he'd managed before, still lagging several yards behind.

"Keep comin'." George chuckled. "Your patients are gonna cheer when they hear them crutches in the ward."

Hadn't thought of it that way. Maybe he's right.

The yellow fire hydrant ahead brought it all back. Dennis's knee wobbled, sweat dampening his back. He crutched on to the next intersection, where George waited to press the crosswalk button.

"I've been stopping at the diner a couple times a week for the last few months. Charlie makes the best hash browns."

"Does he? I used to have a standing order." *This is where I'd stepped between cars when--*

George grinned. "Yup, Charlie and the regulars call it the 'Doc Dennis Special,' black coffee, two eggs scrambled, and whole wheat toast. Rumor has it that yours is permanently on the house."

"I hadn't heard."

"Let's go, we've got the signal." George rolled ahead, definitely on a mission.

The crutch tips sent out gas-filmed splashes with each *tromp* Dennis made. On the other corner, there was more maneuvering room, and he moved beside the wheelchair.

"Is my special a money-maker for Charlie?"

"I know several of his newer customers who choose it. Keep comin'. You're doin' well."

Head down, Dennis paused for breath. "You're easier to please than my therapists." *God, bless the kids on the ward. This'll take longer than I'd hoped.*

"All those kids want is to see that you're back. Quit lookin' at the pavement." George moved on.

At the change in tone, Dennis straightened. He blinked. A large, navy blue awning shaded the diner's windows and the concrete ramp running the full width of its frontage. A woman in a power chair rolled out the door and down the far side, accompanied by her service dog.

"That's Florence. Charlie slips JoJo bacon when they come in." George sped up the ramp. "Now, get a move on. I'm not gonna hold this door forever."

Thump. Rattle. Clink. Repeat. George had the door open wide. Who knew the scent of coffee was an accelerant? Dennis swung through. "Charlie, I'll have my usual."

Charlie turned from the griddle, gaped, and dropped his spatula. "Doc Dennis!"

"And give me a side of hash browns and some of your cherry pie with that."

About the Authors

Our authors are an amazing and varied group. We number among us a mule skinner, a former rodeo rider, an artist, an illustrator, a homeschooler, a talented singer and public speaker, and men and women in ministry. We bring our unique experiences and perspectives to our writing. We hope you've enjoyed it—and would like to learn more about us and writing in the next few pages.

John Davis, born in southern Oklahoma, grew up riding horses, following the rodeo, and wishing he could decide what he wanted to do with his life. Losing a leg to a fallen horse hadn't figured into his plan, but once it was gone, he was told he had fewer choices. It was during one of those challenging days of finding out how much he could do, that he realized he had one option that would allow him to accomplish all he ever dreamed and more. Journaling his adventures had given him an edge. Writing was more than an option, it was a career that blended it all together. Pursuing writing meant living on the edge with a pen in his hand.

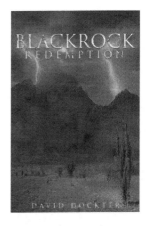 David Dockter grew up in Colorado in the 1960s. Graduating from high school he joined the US Navy serving 4 years active and twelve years reserve. He married his high school sweetheart and has four beautiful kids, losing his love in 2001 after twenty-eight years. Lives in Ordway Colorado and is very active in the church, serving as an elder and a board member. He loves to get out and go camping and fishing whenever he can, mostly in the mountains, where God's creation and beauty can be enjoyed.

Discover David's latest book on Amazon at **www.amazon.com/gp/product/1681971798/**.

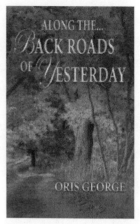

Oris George, the mule writer, captures your heart and soul with his lingering memories of life along the back roads of yesterday. He leaves you with a taste of the time from which he came, a bit of dust on your tongue and a longing in your heart to return. You may not want to live there, but after a glimpse of contentment, you'll want to visit.

Drop by for a visit with Oris George at **www.OrisGeorge.com**.

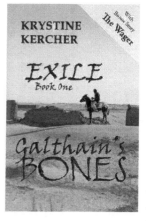

Krystine Kercher is a mother of two, an author and artist, who enjoys sewing and crafting as two of her favorite hobbies. While she has taken on some pretty ambitious projects, she hasn't tried crafting a hot air balloon—yet.

Look for posts about her projects on her author website at **www.KrystineKercher.com** and on her artist website at **www.ContraryMarket.com.**

More Excellent books by Krystine:

Heidi Kortman uses writing to inspire thankfulness because she's witnessed the destructive effects of grumbling. She combats that tendency in her own life by applying thanks even in the most mundane circumstances.

In love with the written, spoken, and sung word from an early age, she has overcome adversity in the form of cerebral palsy to become a gifted singer, talented speaker, and published writer of poems and short stories, and is currently working on several novels. She also loves to sail.

Discover more of Heidi's writing at **www.HeidiDruKortman.com**.

Jude Kandace Laughe was born in the middle of a snow storm, at home. Her parents were unable to get to the hospital, and she believes that ignited a lifetime of arriving a few days earlier than expected. Even for writing deadlines, she arrives a few days early, raring to be published.

She lives in the South Park Valley of Colorado with her daughter Bridgett and their dog Riley. Extensive travels feed her writing efforts and keep her busy home schooling Bridgett, and meeting deadlines.

You'll find a Jude's publications online at **www.writerthoughts.com** and in a variety of magazines and blogs.

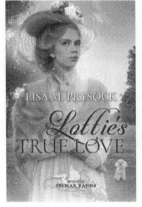

Lisa M. Prysock is an award-winning bestselling Christian and inspirational author of 15 novels. She and her husband of more than 20 years reside in Kentucky. They have five grown children.

She writes Historical Christian Romance and Contemporary Christian Romance novels. She is also the author of a devotional. Lisa enjoys sharing her faith in Jesus through her writing.

Learn more about the author at--: **www.LisaPrysock.com.**

More excellent books from Lisa:

E.V. Sparrow, a writer and illustrator, has served on mission trips, a worship team, and as a prayer ministry leader. She volunteered with Global Media Outreach, and at Serna Village Housing. She also led small groups in Single's, Women's, and Divorce Care ministries. Sparrow's published short stories guide readers to encounter the unexpected.

Discover more about her writing and illustrating at **www.sparrow.world**.

E.V. has also published short stories in:

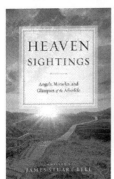

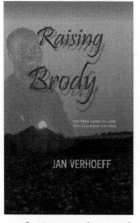

Jan Verhoeff lives for the luster of the dawn, seeks the flavor of goodness, and dares to capture the slice of life that makes happily-ever-after a possibility. Jan searches for ways to share her love of life, family, and country through writing opportunities that come with blogging, writing, and journaling for publication. Whether it's writing a blog post, or writing a book, she finds inspiration in family, travel, and friends.

Come fly with Jan at **www.JanVerhoeff.com**.

More excellent books by Jan:

Mishael Austin Witty lives in Kentucky with her husband, two daughters, and three cats. Her writing brings you through the tensest, messiest human emotions and situations into the most satisfying, realistic conclusions. It shows what God can do in anyone's life, if they let Him. He takes the worst parts of us and turns them into something amazing. There's real hope and healing in the message, and it's something that needs to be shared with the world. Mishael thinks it's part of her mission to do just that. When she isn't writing stories, you'll find her online, volunteering as a Search for Jesus discipleship coach or offline, discipling women who are coming out of the adult entertainment industry.

Explore the goodness of God's grace with Mishael at **www.mishaelaustinwitty.com**.

Made in the USA
Middletown, DE
31 January 2020